NOT JOINED UP

Surviving Retirement
on the Costa del Sol

by

Carole Hart

ISBN 978-1-907407-51-2

THE BLACK LEAF PUBLISHING GROUP
83 Clipstone Rd West
Forest Town, Mansfield
NG190ED
Nottinghamshire
England

www.blackleafpublishing.com

"I know a lot of words, but I can't join them up into sentences.."

Leaving England

Carole Hart

Other books by Carole Hart

Leaving England

Despite its title, Carole Hart's first published book is not about leaving the UK, it is, in fact, about living in Cornwall, in the far South West of England. Carole and her husband Bernie had never previously been to Cornwall, when in 1997 they bought an old cottage in the ancient market town of St Columb Major and set up a small bed and breakfast there. Their attempts at offering a five star experience, in exchange for very little cash, provides us with a funny and interesting story, full of colourful and amazing characters, both living in the town and passing through. Eventually a dramatic turn of events lead to a reassessment of their situation and another departure, this time for Spain.

The Black Leaf Publishing Group

www.blackleafpublishing.com

ISBN 978-1-907407-19-2

Not Joined Up

FOREWORD

There have been many books written about the British who move to Spain. Usually they concern brave souls who live on mountain slopes, with a thousand avocado trees to water, a cesspit, generator, dodgy track and a menagerie of animals. Often these types care very little for those who take the easy way out and buy an apartment on the coast, in fact some actually despise them, criticising them for not integrating, and saying they refuse to learn the language. This may be, in some cases, fair comment, but often these ex-pats are retired and quite elderly and their brains are not wired for the mental gymnastics of studying Spanish grammar. They try, and then they give up.

The reality of living on the Costa lies somewhere between the glossy sunny photos of the ex-pat lifestyle magazines and the more depressing articles of the English language newspapers with their tales of Town Hall corruption, builder incompetence, pick-pocket scams, juvenile cat burglars and bogus gas men. Here is a world apart, of people living British lives in a foreign place, connecting with Spanish customs only when they need to, and then only to those aspects of the Mediterranean lifestyle that still retain their original appeal. Some of them settle well and live happily ever after. Some of them are lonely, some unsettled, but, as in the Blitz, they soldier on, making the most of it, drinking too much, searching for PG Tips and struggling with the heat, the language and the unforgiving bureaucracy. They neither belong to the UK or to Spain, but live in a no-man's land with one foot in each camp. Like their dubious language skills they are not joined up.

This is a story of a mixed bunch of ex-pats living in an imaginary seaside resort in the east of the Costa del Sol, which I have called *Orilla del Mar.* The characters are all entirely fictitious, but, sadly, many of the incidents that befall them, are all too real.

Carole Hart

Chapter One

Accidentally on Purpose

After the wettest Winter in living memory it was no surprise that Orilla del Mar was looking decidedly bedraggled and scruffy. Dirt from roof tiles had streamed down the walls of the apartment blocks leaving long grey streaks, peeling back paint both old and new. The last of the original little houses were running with damp inside and out, their crimped red roofs sprouting moss and grasses. Weeds grew everywhere, in every nook and every damp fuelled cranny. At the corner of her street Pat made a detour to avoid the manhole cover that had popped its iron lid and spilled streamers of filthy toilet paper, turds and other unmentionables across the road.

Pat turned the corner and was pleased to see a few big, battered vans hugging the kerb. The long steep stretch of the main road rose up before her and was bordered with the striped and tarpaulined shacks of the Wednesday market. Because of the torrential downpours of the last two weeks no market had been held, a couple of the most hardy stall holders had attempted to sell vegetables but the majority had stayed away. This had made Pat's heart sink because she hated to admit to herself that market day was now her favourite day. She picked her way slowly around the muddy puddles, avoiding the people

1

pulling shopping trolleys, pushing prams or dragging little dogs. She didn't want to get to the end of it too soon. At the far end it petered out into a few illegal traders and an old man sitting on a sack of his home grown potatoes, holding up fat cloves of pink tinged garlic in a grubby hand. Up ahead was Emilio's café. Emilio was busy wiping the last of the night's rain from his chairs and tables with a cloth. She approached him.

'*Hola*, Emilio..' He turned with that world-weary look of his and his face brightened as he wished her *buenas dias*. He indicated the chair where she always sat, tucked into a corner with a clear view down the market-lined hill. She could see he'd wiped that chair down in readiness. Pat sat there and made a fuss with her bag and her umbrella, not wanting to seem too eager. Emilio asked if she wanted a *café con leche,* and of course, she did. He went inside to fetch it. Since Bob died last year this had become her little treat, having a coffee on market day, hoping to, accidentally on purpose, bump into Keith.

She peered down the hill and yes, there he was! His snow white hair and tidy military moustache stood out in all that grey raincoated crowd. His walk, too, was so familiar, slightly stooped but smart and regular. She watched him without attempting to attract his attention, but when Emilio came with the coffee he blocked her view, and then, suddenly, Keith stood before her.

'Hello, dear lady,' he always called her that, she blushed a little, 'May I?' he asked, indicating the chair next to her, and sat

2

himself down.

'No market for two weeks! I didn't bother coming, did you?' he shook his head, 'Bob used to say if they didn't set the markets up because it was raining in England, they'd never have a market at all!' Keith laughed, in that friendly way of his.

'Indeed!' Emilio came out and asked what he wanted, as if he didn't know, 'A *cortado,*' he confirmed. He was carrying a heavy plastic bag of something, Pat enquired what it was.

'Oranges, for the juice. They are so damned heavy though! Think I'm going to have to change over to the bottled stuff.'

'It's such a messy business, too, squeezing them,' he agreed. There was a nasty gap in the conversation and Pat struggled to fill it before it dried up completely. 'I've heard they've got a new couple in the Marinero, do you go in there at all?'

'Occasionally, not much. Sometimes if Poppy can make it to the end of the Paseo but she doesn't go far these days.' Poppy was his old dog. Pat had never actually seen Poppy, but she had heard all about her.

'I like to go on quiz nights,' she confessed, 'Bob and I used to go, and Geoff, you know Geoff the previous landlord, he said to me, Pat, you must still come to the quiz. They make me ever so welcome. Sometimes I sit with Julie and Roger and as you probably know, they usually win.'

'Perhaps the new man won't have a quiz night,' Keith

3

pondered.

'Oh, I do hope he does, I should miss it so much.' A break in the cloud revealed the sun, and it was such a surprise. Everybody looked up and watched it disappear again behind another, darker, cloud. Still, it augured the promise of Spring.

'I thought it was going to come out!' Keith declared.

'So did I. To think how we complain in the Summer and suffer so, and now we would be so glad to see the end of this rain. Its been just like England.. or Scotland, in your case.'

'Indeed. Not so cold though...'

'True enough.'

* * * * *

As they stepped out of the taxi the sun broke through the clouds. It was an omen, Lynne thought, of the start of a brand new life. While Brian sorted out the luggage and paid the man, Lynne looked skywards at the bright light but it slid away as soon as it had appeared, and the cloud that covered it was as dense as oil. Several cars passed before they could cross the road, one of them splashing through a puddle which narrowly missed her pressed designer jeans. She picked up the lightest of the bags, a holdall, and Brian struggled to manoeuvre the other three cases, which were tottering on their little wheels. Across the road stood the shuttered bar called El Marinero (The Sailor) which they had come here to run. Not that either of

4

them had run a bar before, but it was always Lynne's dream to live in Spain and to offer hospitality in some form and so it seemed the obvious answer. As far as Brian was concerned he had given in to the idea as a last ditch resort, hoping, in making Lynne happy, that it would save their sagging marriage, like a plank shores up an old mattress and gives it a modicum of life.

El Marinero was painted a rather garish shade of sea blue. The heavy metal shutters were pulled down and locked with a giant padlock. To one side there was a Chinese Bazaar shop selling clothes, beach paraphernalia and general hardware and to the other a Spanish-run restaurant called La Abuela (The Grandmother), which was closed and shut up. Wet, dark blue plastic chairs printed with adverts for a type of fizzy water were stacked on one side of the shutters, and tables, with the same brand emblazoned on their tops, stood eight high in a spiral on the other. Brian bent low and produced the keys they'd picked up earlier.

'Good God!' said Lynne, 'There's hundreds of them.. what are they all for?'

'And which one opens the padlock?' a voice in his left ear replied,

'I think it's that one..' and he looked up, startled, to see an odd looking couple bending over his shoulder, 'Yes, that's the one,' said the man. Brian put it into the lock and it fitted, they rolled up the shutter between them while the women watched.

5

The couple introduced themselves.

'I'm Andrea and this is Phillip, such a co-incidence that we were passing by and saw you get out of the taxi..' she explained, unconvincingly. It seemed suspicious, Lynne thought, they must have been waiting to pounce, probably round the corner.

'How come you knew which key to use?' asked Brian.

'Ah, well,' said Phillip, 'We have helped out at times, when Geoff needed to go away on business and so on. All the regulars pull together here, we are a happy bunch.'

'Oh, that's lovely!' said Lynne, casting aside her previous misgivings, ' You must come in and have a coffee or something, our first customers.'

'But we are not open yet,' Brian reminded her, 'Not until Geoff comes round and shows us the ropes.' Phillip obviously didn't think that was needed, he indicated which key opened the door and they all traipsed inside. Lynne had looked forward to this moment for months, she had fancied crossing the threshold on their own, hand in hand, a fresh start. Now it was spoiled.

The smell of stale smoke and beer hit their nostrils, Lynne set about opening up what few windows they had while Brian hauled the cases inside, explaining that they had rented an apartment just a few yards away, but that Lynne wanted to see the bar first. Andrea and Phillip settled into the corner as though it was their own living room.

'Would you like a coffee?' asked Lynne, 'I know I would. On the house.' Brian was behind the bar staring at the huge

6

Gaggia coffee machine.

'Er.. I don't know how to.. not till Geoff....'

'We know how it works..' the customers chorused, 'But it will take twenty minutes or so to fire up...'

'Oh,' said Lynne, 'Well another drink then?'

'Lets have a small brandy!' said Andrea, and Phil nodded,

'Yes, special occasion.' Brian reached up to locate the appropriate glass and took down two small brandy balloons.

'No, not those ones,' Andrea insisted, 'The ones next to them..' He took down the bigger glasses and then scanned the shelves asking which make they preferred, they told him Soberano. He poured a small, English style measure into one glass, at which Andrea advised, 'Keep going, you count to seven...four, five, six....that's it, lovely!' Lynne couldn't believe that anybody could drink such a whopping measure so early in the day. She carried them over to their table.

'Cheers!' they cried as they sipped, then slurped, the drinks. 'Tell me..' asked Phillip, 'What did you do in the UK, then?'

'I was in events management,' said Lynne making it sound very grand, 'I worked for a company that specialised in corporate entertaining.' They were impressed, and Lynne liked to impress. She tidied her jacket and smoothed an imaginary wisp of hair from her forehead.

'And Brian?' they knew their names, it seemed, in advance of being introduced.

7

'Oh Brian was in the Police,' Lynne announced, 'He took early retirement.'

'Hung up my truncheon..' he added. He tried not to give away his rank, better that they thought of him as a Dixon of Dock Green character.

'He was a Detective Sergeant,' said Lynne, 'C.I.D.'

'Oooh! We'll be alright if there are any murders in Orilla del Mar, then..' said Andrea, as though wishing somebody would be found dead.

'I hope there won't be,' said Brian, laughing, 'And if there are I'll leave them to the Guardia to clear up.' He shot Lynne a dirty look, he didn't want everybody to think he was looking into their business, why couldn't she have kept the C.I.D. bit to herself?

Lynne weighed Andrea up, she was always fascinated with appearances. Andrea had long grey hair in a pigtail, reaching to her waist. 'How many years has it been like that?' thought Lynne, 'Probably since she was a child.' It did her no favours. She wore huge glasses with pale frames which made her turned up nose look even shorter. She had a heavy figure loosely covered with a long cardigan over a T shirt and an ankle length zebra printed skirt. And saggy boots. Her bulky square bag was strung across her body like a tram conductor's ticket machine. Phillip, on the other hand, was tall but round shouldered, wearing an ancient tweed jacket with suede patches on the elbows and

8

sleeves too short, a greying white shirt, knee-length kharki shorts with multiple baggy pockets, tan sandals and black socks. The bit of leg between sock and knee was very brown, but his face was pale, with a light grey stubble, and ancient horn rimmed glasses. His thin grey hair hung over his collar.

'Yes,' said Andrea, half way down the brandy by now, 'You'll find us a happy bunch in El Marinero! I - er — hope you will continue with the quiz nights, they are very popular.' Lynne looked pleased,

'Yes, of course, when are they?'

'Monthly, the next one's two weeks on Thursday. You don't have to worry about setting the questions, we regulars do it in turns.'

'I'm next,' said Phillip, 'Got it all ready.'

'Oh, that'll be great,' said Lynne, 'A good chance to meet everybody!'

'They all turn out for the quiz!' Phillip confirmed, 'Sometimes we get ten teams or more if it's fine.'

Lynne's expertise in planning corporate polo matches, setting up cocktail parties and fashion shows was in overtime. She would lay on cheese and wine as a welcome to everybody before the quiz, be generous. She didn't think Brian would go for that, immediately, she'd have to work on him, he didn't want to spend more than he had to until they were turning a profit. He could be a real skinflint at times.

Andrea stood up and pointed to the window which was

9

showing a few droplets of rain.

'Oh, no.. it's raining again, I thought it had finished. Better have another brandy, Brian, and wait until it stops.' Two large empty glasses were placed on the bar. Brian picked up the Soberano and began to wonder what he had let himself in for. After all he was half a bottle of brandy down and they weren't even open yet.

Chapter Two

New Kids on the Block

Julie was early getting to the Hospice Shop on her first day as a volunteer. She wasn't nervous, Julie was not the nervous type, rather she was hoping that this would kick start her integration into the real Spain. They'd lived there for three years, Julie and Roger, in a modern house just slightly up in the *campo,* because she didn't want to live on the coast surrounded by other Brits. She had to admit, and it took a hell of a lot to get her to admit, that choosing the *campo* had been a mistake. Their Spanish neighbours, from Madrid and Córdoba respectively, only came in high summer and that was when Roger insisted that they went back to the UK to visit family and escape the crowds and the oppressive heat. Only Pepe, who farmed the land on the terraces below them, was available for Spanish conversation and he spoke a thick Andalucian dialect which was as totally incomprehensible to Julie as her Castellano Spanish was to him. After five years of night school, tapes and books and learning all she could about Spanish culture, Julie was left half way up a mountain, suffering from vertigo and speaking only to her husband in her mother tongue. She was desperate to integrate.

She found a café opposite the Hospice Shop where she could watch for signs of Maggie, the manageress. Luckily it was the kind of bar she liked, *tipico,* that is dark, noisy and very Spanish. Julie, with her tall slim figure, neat in maroon trousers, shiny patent shoes and crisp white shirt with the collar turned up at the back of her neck, stood out amongst the grimy workmen and Spanish O.A.P.s. She was, apart from the girl in the kitchen, the only woman there. An old man in the corner seemed to be coughing his lungs into a paper serviette. He wrapped his lungs and threw them on the floor. The weak light bulb gave very little illumination and threw strange shadows, while the sun that day was so thin it hadn't yet penetrated the room. She sat at a table near the door and waited for the waiter to come over. But he gave her a look which said 'bloody tourist' so she got up and went to the bar. The counter was lined with rows of thick little glasses standing on white saucers, each with two sachets of sugar and a spoon, ready for the breakfast rush. Each spoon was at the same angle, each sugar packet on the left side, logo up. The coffee machine, a double sized monster, hissed and growled and whistled. The men raised their voices accordingly, grunting to each other and shouting in the same thick *Andaluz* as Pepe the farmer. She couldn't pick out a word.

She raised her voice and shouted.

'Leche manchada y pan tostado con sobresada..' To say the barman was impressed would be understating it. He was not just impressed that she had some knowledge of Spanish and a

12

flawless pronunciation, but flabbergasted at an order so different for an *extranjero,* a foreigner. They only ever ordered *café con leche* and toast with butter. Or beer.

Julie went and sat down. The men at the next table were reading from a football newspaper and drinking thick black coffee in chunky glasses. Two of them were painters, in white overalls splashed with ochre coloured paint, and the other two were builders with strong tanned legs, cut off jeans, big boots and clean, but old, T shirts. They eyed her suspiciously, her general tidiness, her brown hair twisted and clamped on top of her head with a mock tortoiseshell grip. The floor was littered with papers, serviettes, cigarette butts, sugar sachets; she knew that it was the custom to sweep up periodically. The barman brought her order and she paid, to save time. She tore the top off the sugar sachet and put just a few grains into her drink, but then, too English to throw the sachet on the floor, she tidied up by putting the torn off strip inside the packet and put it into the clean glass ashtray. With one eye on the Hospice Shop she started to eat the toasted roll.

It wasn't that Julie liked *sobresada* particularly, or indeed preferred the weak *leche manchada* (literally translating as 'stained milk') to the more ordinary types of coffee, but here in the Malaga province there were twelve types of coffee served and she had to choose the most unusual.

She had barely picked at her bread and sipped her drink when a woman, small and with an impatient air about her,

13

started unlocking the shop opposite. They had only spoken on the phone, but Julie had seen her around the shop when she went in looking for books, and now realised that she was Maggie. Hurriedly she left the bar and crossed the road. The woman turned towards her. She had the most amazing nectarine coloured hair, red, yellow and black all at once, standing up in bizarre spikes above an ordinary middle aged face with gold rimmed glasses.

'Hello, I'm Julie..'

'Ah, yes, you're early. I'm afraid it's not a good start for you, Judy..'

'Julie..'

'Sorry, Julie. You see Liz and Maribel have both rung me, Maribel can't come today and Liz has to take her dog to the vets so she is going to be late. Just you and me at the moment. You do know the shop don't you?'

'Well, yes, I'm often in here looking for books and sometimes DVD's for my husband.'

'You do speak Spanish, don't you?' Julie nodded, 'And German?'

'No, not German,' Julie wasn't expecting that. Maggie shrugged.

'Fair enough.' She hauled up the shutters revealing rails stuffed with clothes. Julie, personally, would never consider buying second-hand clothes. There was a faint musty smell of mould mixed with sweat hanging round the garments that put her

14

right off.

'Help me wheel these outside, watch your back, they're heavy..' As they wheeled the rails out Maggie lamented, 'Of course that's the trouble with volunteers, they've no compunction to turn up. Bloody dog needs the vet, grandchildren visiting, not feeling well and they let you down at the drop of a hat. That's why we've such a turnover of staff. Have you been affected directly?'

'Pardon? By what?'

'By that bloody disease that makes it necessary for us to have a Hospice at all! Cancer, I mean. Not many people haven't had some experience of it..'

'Well, no.. I haven't had direct experience.'

'You are bloody lucky then. You did realise that this is what the shop's about, raising money for the Cancer Care Hospice?'

'Oh, yes, of course.'

'Well, I'll be going 'backstage', in the sorting room, and turning out the latest collection of designer goodies that the public have donated. You stand there, keep an eye out for thieves, there's plenty of them about, I can tell you. If you sell anything the money is in that cash box under the counter. All the clothes are marked, books are one euro, DVD's are two and VHS tapes are only fifty cents. Alright?'

So Maggie, an Englishwoman with a bizarre taste in hairstyles, went behind the curtain leaving Julie on her own. No customers, no Spanish assistants to talk to, and, so far, nothing to do.

* * * * *

The storm that night was the worst since Christmas Eve, and even angels from the Realms of Glory would not have considered going out on that night. Huge horizontal plains of light flashed across the little town, the wind howled and danced, tearing down half hung posters, ripping off whole branches, tossing the pink and purple bracts of bougainvillea into the air like giant confetti, lifting empty cardboard boxes to the height of lamp posts. Rain lashed already sodden walls and drummed against glass whilst the thunderclaps shook the damp foundations of the buildings, rattled the window blinds and heralded the most ferocious bolts of lightning, which struck the distant sea with a hiss and almost parted the waves. Pat, who was a timid person at the best of times, didn't like thunder, and spent a sleepless night hugging a pillow and wishing that Bob was there to get her through it. Eventually she dozed off for an hour but was awoken by the sound of her neighbour's grandfather clock. Through the thin wall she counted the chimes, seven of them. So she knew it was about 9.30. She had long since realised that the market would definitely be off, so, to try and cheer herself up, she decided to brave the rain, which had now become a blustery drizzle, and walk the seafront promenade, known as the Paseo, to the Marinero bar at the far end. There, she could check if the quiz was still on and meet the new owners.

The damage the storm had done to the beach was unbelievable. The river, usually a tame (if not completely dried up) stream had swollen to a raging torrent and brought down from the mountain heaps of rubbish. This was once a sugar cane growing area and that plant spreads like a weed especially in river beds where it can grow up to forty feet in height if unchecked. The water ripping at its roots had dislodged all the dry broken canes, pulled out huge bushes and sent them hurtling down to the sea. On the way they had picked up broken plastic chairs, supermarket trolleys, concrete blocks, a telegraph pole and pieces of wood the size of tea chests. All this bobbed out to sea and then came back on the surf to pile up on the beach. Heaps of vegetation and other rubbish were eight foot high everywhere. Spanish people, who detest the wind at the best of times, had braved it to come down and point saying, '*Ay-eee, Semana Santa!*' as Easter, *(Semana Santa)* was only two weeks away and it was an unwritten law that the Council had the beach looking immaculate for the first of the season's visitors.

Brian was settling in to life in the bar. It had seemed strange at first, he had to admit, but now he had mastered the coffee machine and found where everything was kept he was beginning to enjoy it. Lynne, whose culinary talents didn't reach

17

far at the best of times, was coping with bacon sandwiches, full English breakfasts and beans on toast. Brian was coming to terms with the regulars, and their patterns of attendance. People, he knew, were creatures of habit, and these creatures were definitely running to type.

At about ten thirty every day Andrea and Phil would come in for their morning coffee with a brandy chaser, then Mick and Sandra. Mick was a big man, tall and heavy who walked with his shoulders held back and sat with his huge thighs splayed apart. Lynne was worried that the plastic chair wouldn't take his weight, but so far, so good. According to Andrea, Mick was known as "Mr Wikipedia" as he considered himself the font of all knowledge. Sandra's main purpose in life was to stop him in his tracks and rubbish him whenever she could. Later Malcolm and Jenny might drop in. Malcolm had a similar bulk to Mick and the two would sit on either side of the room, facing each other, like Toby Jugs holding court. The fact they they didn't like each other was pretty easy to see, as they would contradict each other's pomposity at every turn. Jenny, a mousey little woman who never said a thing, would sit in a corner and read, leaving Sandra to referee. Malcolm wore a leather Stetson type hat over his bald pate which earned him the nickname of Crocodile Dundee.

That day Roger, Julie's husband, turned up and sat at the bar. Brian liked Roger, he was a normal sort of bloke, inoffensive, good humoured and laid back. He hadn't met Julie yet.

'Have you seen the state of the beach?' Roger asked everybody.

'Shocking!' said Malc, 'They'll never get it straight for Easter.'

'I don't know why they bother trying,' Mick added, 'Last year they spent thousands carting away all that rubbish and on Good Friday it rained again and we got another lot.'

Roger ordered a coffee.

'My wife's just started as a volunteer in the Hospice Shop.' Roger explained over the noise of the machine.

'Oh, where's that then?'

'At the other end of town, behind the Hotel.'

'I haven't had time to get to know the town yet,' Brian confessed.

'Don't suppose you have.' Brian handed the coffee over..

'Where do you live, then, Roger?'

'Up the *campo*.'

'What does that mean "up the *campo*"? People keep saying it and I haven't the first idea what they are talking about,' he whispered.

'It means out of town, in the countryside. Round here that translates as up the mountains.'

'Are you very high up, then?'

'No, not as the crow flies. But then crows don't follow the roads, do they? The roads are all dangerous bends and sheer

19

drops. It takes half an hour or so.'

'And your wife, doesn't she drive?'

'Oh, Julie drives alright. She has no fear of driving to the airport, even of driving in Málaga city, but she can't cope with the mountain roads. Doesn't like having to pull over to the edge when a lorry comes towards her. She gets vertigo if she looks down the drop. So I'll be back tonight to pick her up.'

Pat came through the door, shaking her brolly behind her, and asked,

'Have you seen the state of the beach? There's even one of those big cable drum things on there, you know like giant cotton reels, and a telegraph pole!'

'We were just saying.' said Sandra, nodding. Mick drew breath ready to impart his knowledge.

'Those cable drums were left all over the valley by Sevillana, the Electricity Company when they first connected up the farms in the *campo.* They left them everywhere and the Spanish collected them up and used them for dining tables and all sorts, they never let anything go to waste.'

'Bit like you then,' said Sandra, 'Tight wads.' Mick ignored this.

Andrea was trying to get Pat to sit with them but she declined, politely, she knew it was fatal, you could never get away. She went and sat next to Roger, whom she liked, he had been very kind when Bob died.

Lynne came out of the kitchen carrying two plates of

20

bacon sandwiches. She was wearing a fitted white cotton overall.

'Bloody hell!' said Malc, 'I thought this was a pub not a dentist's.'

'What do you mean? This is a proper cook's overall, I thought it looked hygienic.'

'I think it looks very hygienic,' said Pat, and Lynne smiled at her, she liked her immediately.

'Thank you,' she said, putting the food in front of Mick and Sandra.

'That'll be too hot in the Summer,' Andrea advised and Phil agreed,

'You'll never stand it. There's no air in that kitchen, one lot of chips and the place is like a furnace. You mark my words.'

Mick joined in, taking a bite of his sandwich and laying it aside.

'That kitchen wouldn't pass muster in England. Not like that with no ventilator,' he took another bite then added, 'You do realise that you will have to take a Health and Safety in the Kitchen exam in order to get your Food Handling Certificate?'

'No... what, in Spanish?' Lynne looked terrified.

'Yep! It's the law.' Andrea confirmed this.

'Don't worry Lynne, Diane at The Meeting Place took it last year. She said it was a piece of cake.'

'Do they have a translator?'

'Better than that, they give you the answers. They tell you which boxes to tick so everybody passes.'

21

'What's the point of that, then?'

'It makes them look good to have a hundred per cent pass rate I suppose.'

Chapter Three

Quiz Night

Mrs Gonzales hosed down the pavement in front of her house every day of her life. Even when the Council had dug it up once and left a heap of rubble and broken tarmac in its place for weeks, she still hosed it down with a thick bore hosepipe, letting it pour for a good twenty minutes. She was completely oblivious to dire warnings of drought in the Summer, and to rain in Winter. This was what she did, usually whilst wearing her pyjamas and dressing gown, day in, day out and she always would.

Pat skirted around the spouting hosepipe and nodded *'Buenas dias,'* to her neighbour as she passed. It would be nice, she thought, if she could say more than that to her, but she didn't know how. Pat had a spring in her step that day, the market would definitely be on, and, hopefully, she could re-unite with Keith. The sun was shining and the sky was a heavenly blue, in other words back to normal.

Walking through the market was still a delight. She loved the bright displays of fruit and veg., how it changed with the seasons. Right now it was fat strawberries and spring onions the size of oranges, later it would be black cherries and dark red peppers as sweet as apples. Melons, like striped rugby balls

23

and watermelons the size of classroom globes, slashed to reveal moist crimson flesh, came in the height of summer. She loved the colourful dresses of the African women, the racks of T shirts and heaps of jumbled clothes you could pick through. She loved the cries of the traders, 'Special price!' *'Barato, barato!'* Pat loved the record man who always played the same CD and the South American Indian girls, short and round, with long glossy hair and lacy blouses, their pretty children playing under the stalls and round their feet. The tall black African men selling sunglasses and jewellery reminded her of something Bob used to say, 'The missionaries went to Africa and traded baubles and beads, now they are selling them back to us!' and he would laugh at that. There were the Moroccans with shoes and leather goods, spices and herbs and of course Spanish people and gypsies selling honey, figs, fruit, vegetables and Chinese made clothes. Always something different, it always brought a smile to her face.

At the end of the market was Tomato Man, she hadn't seen him for weeks. This little old man with a strange twisted face and a big ball of flesh hanging from his ear lobe like a dangling hairy golf ball was a local feature. Loaded with misshapen tomatoes on a wheelbarrow he would walk miles to market, set up a little wonky plastic scales which looked like they came from a toy box, balance as many big tomatoes on it as he could, charge you a euro then throw in six more. People bought from him to help him out, rumour had it that he lived in a hovel

24

with no roof, running water or sanitation.

Keith was already in Emilio's, he had already had his coffee. The smile on his face was as broad as hers, it seemed months since they had met. She sat beside him, she felt giddy, like a silly girl.

'Haven't seen you my dear,' he said, 'I came last week but I suppose it was too wet for you.' She couldn't believe he had turned out in that storm.

'Oh, yes, I am sorry, I didn't think...' She could kick herself for not coming, she wanted to ask for his phone number so that it wouldn't happen again but thought that a bit forward. She ordered her coffee. 'How have you been'?

'Fine, fine. Stuck in rather more than I'd like. Just took Poppy round the gardens.'

'Oh, well you are lucky there, you have such lovely gardens at the Bella Vista apartments. Ours are..well..nothing special.'

'Esteban, my neighbour, came round a couple of times for a game of chess. That was very pleasant.' She wished, for the first time in her life, that she knew how to play.

'I called into El Marinero. The new people seem nice and the quiz is on as usual..'

'Have you seen the state of the beach?' She nodded, with the familiar comment,

'And it's almost Semana Santa.' When she was with him she felt different, more relaxed. More like she used to feel when

25

she was with Bob, more her old self. She just wished she could get a little closer, be on more familiar terms than this, but she didn't want to frighten him away.

* * * * *

Lynne had it all planned. On entering they would be greeted at the door and offered a glass of sparkling wine and a *canapé,* she had spent all afternoon preparing dainty morsels, things on sticks, cheese on little crackers, Serrano ham rolled around stoned olives. Brian thought this a mistake but let her get on with it. He thought this crowd were more pork dripping than paté, more Spam than Serrano, and hoped they would appreciate the trouble she had taken. He'd tried to warn her but she wouldn't have it, sweating away in the tiny kitchen boiling quails' eggs and stuffing mini vol au vents. As the day went on the weather had worsened until by seven o'clock there was a howling wind. Every few minutes Lynne would go to the door and check on the sky, holding her hand out as a test for rain. If the weather was too bad, would they come?

She needn't have worried, curiosity driven, they rolled up in their droves.

Andrea and Phillip came first, no surprise there, so that they could grab their usual table, Phillip clutching the all important questions under his arm, guarding them from prying eyes. Andrea assured everybody that she had had no sight of

26

the questions or their answers, and was therefore available to make up a team. Then Roger and Julie arrived accompanied by Pat, as Roger had picked her up on the way. They settled at a table to make a team of three. Then came Mick and Sandra, Malc (Jenny never came to the quiz), a large man called Dan and a very small Scotsman known as "Big Mac" with his wife and sullen looking daughters. Finally a few people that nobody knew, four friends sharing a holiday apartment and two married couples who had a house in the *campo*. Each was greeted by a beaming Lynne and offered wine and nibbles but a lot of them declined, looking at her as though she was a paedophile offering sweets to a child. There was a great deal of shuffling of tables and chairs and getting drinks in before everyone was settled. Lynne raised her voice and welcomed everybody.

'I'm Lynne and this is Brian, thank you for joining us at the Marinero and please help yourself to more *canapés* here on the table, thank you.'

Phil got up and positioned himself somewhere in the middle of the room and then started handing out photocopies for the picture round, which was famous faces for identification. It was at that point when the lights all went out and a shriek of 'Whoa!' went up.

'Power cut, don't anybody move!' cried Mick, 'I know where the fuse box is, it has probably flipped the switch..' The noise of somebody getting to their feet and bumping into furniture was suddenly joined by the crash of glass onto tile. The lights

27

blinked on and everybody stared at the pile of smashed champagne glasses and plates full of dainties that were under the size 12 feet of Mick Underwood. Lynne shrieked and went to get a brush and pan.

'Oh, what a shame!' cried Pat, 'All your dainty...' (she was stuck for the right word. Bob would have said "horse's doofers" but she wasn't sure that was right) '...so much work and they are all on the floor!'

It was too late to salvage anything, Mick was, for once, quite apologetic, and everybody clucked in unison as to 'what a pity but it was an accident'. Phil cleared his throat and started the quiz.

The first round was called Highdays and Holidays. Question one was 'Which holiday is known in Spain as *Semana Santa?*' This was an easy one to kick off with Phil had thought. Question two was 'What do the Spanish eat with their Christmas turkey?'

Mick shouted out 'Chips, they eat chips with everything,' at which everybody laughed. Then Dan suggested it was winkles in batter, and somebody else proposed pickled garlic. Amid the laughter one of the strangers tugged Phil's sleeve.

'Excuse me, but are all the questions going to require a knowledge of Spain and Spanish? We come from Wolverhampton, we are only here for a bloody fortnight, how are we supposed to know all these things about Spain?' she asked.

28

During round two, the Food and Drink round, a few more people came in but said they didn't want to play. One of them stood behind Malc and when the question was posed 'From which Country do red onions originate?' he bent down and whispered in Malc's ear,

'Cyprus. I know its Cyprus because my brother lives there.'

'Are you sure?' he nodded, then turned his back so that people didn't think he was giving away secrets. Malc's team put Cyprus. But the answer was Italy. After three rounds Phil announced,

'We'll break now for the refreshments, then we'll check the first three rounds afterwards.' Lynne, who had been sitting dejectedly on a bar stool, suddenly pricked up her ears.

'Refreshments?' she asked Brian, 'Nobody said anything about...' The conversations now were so noisy that Brian had to ring a bell to make them hear.

'I'm sorry, folks but nobody told us about refreshments, you all saw that Lynne went to a lot of trouble with the canapés, she hasn't prepared any other refreshments, as such...' There were groans and tutting all over the room.

'But we usually have cheese and pickle sandwiches,' said Mick, ungratefully.

'And pork pies, cut up..' said Sandra.

'And sometimes we have sausage rolls..' added Big Mac.

'You should have told us then, what do you think we are,

psychic?' Lynne screamed. Brian could see she was about to boil, he knew that once her mercury started to rise there was no stopping it.

'Never mind,' said Phil, self importantly, 'I suppose it's my fault, as quizmaster I should have filled you in.'

'I'll have a packet of crisps, Brian,' said Sandra, 'Cheese and onion.' Brian threw her the packet and she caught it deftly.

'Oh, no,' said Mick, 'You'll breathe them all over me. You do realise, I hope, that all crisp flavours are totally synthetic?'

'So what?' said Sandra ripping the bag open.

'It's rubbish you are eating, woman!'

'Good, anything you don't like is good enough for me. Give me another packet, Brian, I'll eat them in bed.'

The quiz ended with a general knowledge round. One of the questions was 'What is the famous dessert of Mongolia?' When it came to reading out the answers at the end, Phil realised he had made a mistake. The answer was 'Gobi'.

'Gobi?' said Malc, 'I put rancid yak's yoghurt.'

'I put camel cake..' said somebody else.

'He meant DESERT, not DESSERT...' exclaimed Julie, and everybody laughed but for one stern faced woman in the holidaymakers' team.

'Scrub that question, null and void!' said Phil, 'I'm sorry about that..'

'Excuse me,' said the woman, it was the same one who

had complained about everything being Spanish, 'I got it right.'

'How could you? I read it out wrong, I said...'

'I know what you said,' she interrupted, 'I just knew that you meant desert, I got it right...Gobi.'

'Oh, OK then, you can have the point..'

'No!' said Mick, 'You said it was null and void, so null and void it is.'

'I got it right! Makes up for all those Spanish questions..' Brian stepped in.

'I'm sorry, but I think it's fair if it's taken out of the equation.'

'For all you know,' said Malc, stirring it, 'There is a pudding called Gobi...and it could be made of rancid yak's yoghurt...in which case I got it right as well.'

Lynne slid quietly off her stool and whispered to Brian, 'I'm going home..'

'Good idea', he said, and she went to get her coat.

When it was all over some of them hung around drinking until 2am. Eventually Brian encouraged them to leave and got out a mop and bucket, stacking the chairs on the tables to make sure that there was no glass or canapés clinging to the floor. As he mopped he thought of Andrea's claim that they were 'a friendly bunch', it seemed far from it. He chuckled to himself. Still, he felt sorry for Lynne, she had put a lot of work in and not many had even thanked her for it. Trouble with Lynne was she

31

had a hair trigger, and she could fly off the handle in minutes or drop to a quiet despair. He could read her well enough after thirty-two years of marriage. He was miles away in thought considering all these things when a woman pushed past him and swayed on her spindly heels over to the bar where she pulled her skinny backside onto a stool. She had thin legs clad in tight black jeans, and stunning long glossy hair, straight and ink black, fell down to her waist. Before he could say anything she spoke,

'Cuba Libre, darling.' Putting his mop aside he went behind the bar and faced her, and almost jumped with shock. The tight jeans, lovely hair and high heels hadn't prepared him for the wrinkled, world weary face with eyes outlined with smudgy kohl and red lips drawn round with a purple line.

'Sorry?'

'Cuba Libre!' she raised one fist in a mock salute, 'Rum and coke, darling. No ice.'

He poured her the drink in the usual Spanish way, with the rum half way up the long glass topped off with coke. She drank like she had just crawled across the Sahara, gulping half of it in one. She pushed the correct money towards him.

'Actually, I was just closing..'

'Won't be long, darling.' She finished the drink. His mop clattered to the floor and he started at the noise but she seemed not to notice. 'Nighty, night...' she climbed down from the stool and sashayed out of the door. He quickly pulled the shutters down and looked for his keys. Who *was* that? Was she on the

32

game? Was she drunk?

It was Trish.

Chapter Four

Buttercups and Daisies

When she looked in the mirror the woman she saw looked exactly the same as she always had. In Trish's mind, that is. A slim, young girl in tight black jeans, with luscious long straight hair falling in glossy curtains either side of a pale face. She didn't see the ravages of time, the damage done by lifestyle and decay. She didn't see the wrinkles, the papery thin skin, the age spots that had appeared on her arms and hands. All she saw was the smudgy black eye-liner, loads of mascara and a bright pink mouth. Her make-up and her hairstyle had not changed at all since she was 16, and now she was 63. The only concession to modernity was the lip liner, which she had had tattooed on to save time, choosing a shade of purple which she considered would go with pinks or reds and so be completely dual purpose. You just had to fill it in, like a colouring book.

In the sixties she had run away from boarding school with two friends and they formed a three girl singing group called "The Buttercups". They toured with most of the headliners of the day, living a Rock 'n' Roll lifestyle, drinking, smoking, dabbling with drugs and sleeping with all and sundry. They never had a hit themselves but did mostly backing work and they were good at it. Wild times! She had even slept with one of the Rolling

Stones, but because she was off her head on pot, she couldn't remember which one. Great days! But then the band broke up, Sheila married a dentist and went to live in Hemel Hempstead and Joyce set up an animal sanctuary in Aberdeen. At that point she went home to Daddy, a Harley Street Orthopaedic Surgeon who welcomed her back and forgave her her trespasses, and set her up in a little second-hand book shop off the Old Kent Road. This she ran successfully until Daddy died leaving her a house worth half a million.

After putting it on the market she decided, one day, on the spur of the moment, to catch a bus to Spain. She boarded at London Victoria Station with a guitar she couldn't play and a small holdall full of black jeans with matching T shirts. She intended to stay on the bus until Marbella, a place she had always wanted to go, but her bony backside ached and she had had enough when twenty-seven hours later they reached Orilla del Mar for a "rest stop". She got off the bus and checked into the imaginatively named "Hotel Orilla del Mar", stayed one night, crossed the road and went into a car hire shop run by a guy called Paco. She had the intention of hiring a car and driving the rest of the way, but Paco, who spoke near perfect English, suggested she stay a while in Orilla, he had a small flat he was trying to let above his shop and she could have it for a song. She had been there ever since.

Trish had made the place her own. The walls were painted purple and the windows were hung with voile, dyed purple to match and bravely trimmed with red pom-pom braid. The pseudo crystal chandelier was augmented with black jet beads and strings of pearls, and there were lace cloths draped over all the lampshades. There were a lot of ornate mirrors. Throws, in crimson velvet and damask, were tossed on bed and chair. The decor was a cross between bordello and Victorian parlour. It was a small, dark flat with a tiny bathroom, kitchenette, one bedroom and the square living room where the only window looked out onto the main road. She had her own entrance up the stairs at the side of the shop and her own front door. She kept it very clean and tidy, though she wasn't there much to make any kind of mess. And as for Paco, he still had the car hire shop down below. When he had persuaded her to stay rather than hire a car from him she had assumed he fancied her. Trish always assumed that men fancied her, though these days they rarely did. Paco had never made a move towards her, which she found surprising, but it was more surprising that she had never worked out that he was gay.

She didn't do drugs any more, the only Coke she ingested now was black and fizzy and served with copious amounts of white rum. She no longer smoked pot, only evil smelling Spanish cigarettes. Trish didn't miss any of these things, she was content with her half a million pounds nicely invested and a modest place to live. There was only one thing that she missed from her glory days; it wasn't fame, it wasn't the thrill of performing live, it was sex. She desperately needed physical love. And she wasn't getting any.

* * * * *

Now that the rains seemed to have stopped the Spring could finally begin. The most beautiful aspect of the green Spanish Spring was the buttercups and daisies. Not the tiny weeds that infest English lawns, but Bermuda buttercups with long, graceful stems bursting with sunny yellow flowers. They rose, about a foot high, from mounds of delicate clover-like leaves and grew out of cracks in every rock and pavement. They sprouted from hedgerows, roadsides, river beds. They decorated roadworks, heaps of broken tarmac, rubbish tips and even the beach.   The municipal flowerbeds which were always more sparsely planted than their British counterparts (as the Spanish seemed to like to look at bare soil) were suddenly filled to bursting with golden buttercups and their friends the crown daisies all holding hands with scarlet geraniums and pink petunias.   The daisies had dark green, tough, lacy leaves and stiff stems with flower heads about two inches across. Some were yellow, some white, some bicolour. Spanish gardeners would grub them out, or spray them with weed-killer but they always came back again, stronger.

From Julie's terrace, as she looked down the mountain road towards the coast, she could see a sea of yellow and white

37

along the edges of the road, under the reddish-tinged floppy leaves of the avocado trees, between the rocks in the stream and everywhere that the buttercups and daisies could take hold. It always took her breath away.

The main aspect that had sold Roger and Julie their house in the *campo* was the view. They, like many before them and many more to come, had fallen for that panoramic vista of sea and mountains never affordable to British folk unless they were millionaires. To think they could wake up to this, as the property TV shows often illustrated, to think they could sit on the terrace sipping a glass of wine as the sun set over the silver horizon. Well, they could now. But they didn't, well, only on Sundays.

On Sundays Roger would get the car out and drive down to the coast, there being no shops whatsoever near their house, he would buy warm bread, *vino tinto* and the Sunday Times and bring them back up the mountain again where Julie would be cooking a roast chicken or some other delicious lunch. After they had eaten they would sit together in twin wicker chairs out on the terrace and read the paper, dividing up its copious supplements between them. It was the time of the week they both loved most of all. Roger would read all the sports reports; he loved all sports, football, rugby, cricket and golf. At first Julie wouldn't agree to having English satellite TV, she said they should watch Spanish, but after a few months of watching endless discussion programmes where an overly made-up woman held court with a mixed bunch of people discussing, for hours, the same boring topic, she gave in and they now had Sky.

Julie would read the theatre reviews, particularly the ballet. She could look at a photo of a ballerina and be transported back to Covent Garden. She could drink in the beauty of every curve and line, the effortless effort involved, whether it was the power of a Carlos Acosta *gran jêté*, or the sublime knotting of two bodies in a *pas de deux*. Just looking at them was heaven. It transported her back to those wonderful nights at the Garden, the delicate swell of the full orchestra, the magical sets of fairy castles, misty lakes and floating swans. Or to the strong, modern ballets of Kenneth Macmillan, such as Manon, about prostitution and debauchery. She remembered sitting next to a young man from the Royal Ballet School. He wore skin tight jeans and his muscular structure was as sharply defined as it would be on an anatomical model. West End theatre and the ballet was the only thing that she missed.

* * * * *

When Malcolm walked into the Marinero that morning with Jenny in tow, Brian was taken by surprise. The order in which people had turned up that day had changed; Andrea and Phil were there but Mick hadn't yet showed. Malcolm that day had an extra swagger to his walk, as though he was more full of himself than usual, and he plonked himself down in the chair

39

usually favoured by Mick which, Brian thought, would not go down well at all. Lynne checked that they required the usual order and went into the kitchen while Brian dealt with the mugs of tea.

'Big day today,' Malcolm announced,' Community Meeting Day.'

'Oh, right.'

'Did I tell you I was the President of our block, the Alta Vista?'

'You might have mentioned it.' He'd mentioned it about a hundred times. Malcolm took off his Crocodile Dundee hat and put it on a chair beside him. He swayed back in the chair, stressing its fragile legs.

'Oh, yes. Been President for five years now. Fine old mess it was in before I took over, I can tell you.'

At that point Mick and Sandra arrived, they didn't seem startled to see him in "their" seats.

'Community Meeting Day?' asked Mick, matter-of-factly, and found another table.

'Oh, I hate those meetings,' said Andrea, and Phil agreed, 'The first few years' meetings were hell, everybody speaking Spanish, all at the same time, I couldn't follow what was going on, no sort of order or anything. Then I found out you are entitled to a translator and since then it's not been too bad.. still dread them though.' Lynne came through with the bacon sandwiches, she had been so confident that the four rounds of

40

bacon would be required that she had had it all ready, she handed them out.

'So what are these meetings for?' she asked in all innocence. Brian thought that was fatal, she would get them going now.

'It's the Horizontal Law,' said Mick and Lynne looked puzzled, '*El Ley Horizontal*'

'I'm no nearer..'

'It refers to how Communities work. Your Community being all the people in a given block of flats or on a development. They have to have a President and a Vice President and appoint an impartial Administrator, to handle the money and such.'

'That's right,' said Malcolm. With a look that said I know more about it than you.

'But why is it horizontal and not vertical?' asked Lynne, perplexed. Neither of them knew and they both struggled to come up with a reason.

'It means across the board..' said Malcolm, drawing an imaginary line with the flat of his hand. Mick had to have his say.

'Sort of, It's more like, well, it relates to the floor plan of the *edificio,* that is the block, it indicates that it covers the whole area.' He was proud of that.

'Bollocks!' said Sandra, choking on her bacon sandwich, 'You made that up!' Malcolm carried on regardless.

'Once I took over it improved our meetings no end. For

example..' Andrea and Phil seemed to take this as a kind of signal, put money on the bar and left. Malcolm didn't hesitate, 'We have it out on the terrace, I lay out chairs and tables with glasses of water. I stick to a strict agenda, no messing. Everybody gets ten minutes to speak and they have to tell me in advance what the subjects are. Usually they complain about the cleaner, the gardener or something not working properly, like the lift. Then I sum it all up and the administrator reads out the figures. Who owes, that sort of thing, and tells us what the charges will be for the next year. It's all over and done with by 9.30 sharp. Before I took over they used to go on for hours, till it was dark, and one year...' Mick finished Malc's story that he'd heard so many times.

'...You had to go and get a hurricane lamp because the Administrator couldn't see to read.' Malc was annoyed that Mick had pinched his punch line. Sandra tried to change the subject,

'I hear that the Council have closed down the car boot, say it's unfair competition with the shops. And they are trying to ban the lookey-lookey men.'

'No!' said Lynne, 'I like the lookey-lookey men, they're harmless enough.'

'I hear that another rubber boatload of African illegals came in down the coast the other night, when there was a full moon. Apparently they hit some rocks and had to swim for shore.'

'Should have had a lookey-lookey-out man!' suggested

42

Brian. Malc and Mick took a minute to get the joke, then they both laughed, but it didn't stop the President's address.

'As I was saying, ' said Malcom, 'Before I took over...' Mick got up.

'Come on Sandra, this won't do, we've got to go to the Town Hall about... you know..'

'What?'

'YOU KNOW!' They both got up and left. Brian wished he could go with them.

Chapter Five

Cultures

The Hospice Shop was heaving with customers. Julie and Liz were behind the counter, Maggie was sorting in the back room and Maribel was in charge of hanging the new things on the racks. Until she had worked here Julie had no idea how many nationalities there were in Orilla del Mar. Apart from Spanish and British there were Germans, Scandinavians, Russians, a few French, a lot of Moroccans and an equal number of Senegalese. And today, they all seemed to be here at once. Liz was being firm with a Moroccan man who wanted to reduce the price of some children's toys.

'No, lo si-ento. No cam-bi-ar. Los prec-ios son fij-ados..'
Her Spanish wasn't bad but it was hampered by a Manchester accent. He wouldn't give in. This part of the job Julie hated. What was it that they couldn't understand? It was a charity shop, for God's sake! Liz did very well and stood her ground. The guy went off without the goods. In a brief break in trade Julie congratulated her.

'I hate that. There are notices everywhere, even in Arabic, saying "No bargaining, prices are fixed" yet they still try it on.' Liz agreed, shrugging,

'You just have to accept that it is their culture.' A poor

44

excuse, Julie thought.

'That's not what I'd call it.'

A beautiful tall black African lady with a tiny baby strapped to her back came to the counter with a bright tablecloth marked two euros. She offered them one euro. Julie explained in Spanish that the prices were non-negotiable, at which the lady shrugged and paid up. Generally, they were OK, the Senegalese, they were usually polite and pleasant. And most of them were really poor, trying to scratch a living from selling pirate DVD's and counterfeit Rayban sunglasses so that they could send money home to support desperate relatives.

An Englishwoman came rushing through the shop pushing what looked like a new state of the art three wheeled pushchair, the kind that can be used for a new baby and later for a toddler.

'Can't stop, on a yellow..would you like this, it's almost brand new?'

'Thank you!' said Julie and took it from her. 'How much do we put on this?' she asked Liz, 'I know for a fact that these cost at least two hundred pounds and it's in perfect condition.'

'I don't know. Twenty?' Twenty seemed ridiculously cheap but then it wouldn't sell if they asked more. She thought about checking with Maggie but Maggie was on her mobile talking loudly to somebody who wanted to leave a deposit on the radiogram that had no record deck. Julie was writing a ticket for the pushchair when a young Moroccan girl came up to her.

'How much?'

'Twenty.' She shook her head. In Spanish Julie explained that it was in very good condition and cost more than two hundred new. The girl was unimpressed but continued to examine it. Julie dare not take her eyes off her, only last week somebody had run off with a push bike, and nobody had seen it go. The girl wandered off to find her mother. Then, as they were bagging up a load of clothes for a man who they knew would sell them on the car boot, she came back.

'*Deposito*?' Julie said she would accept a deposit of five euros but she had to collect the item by the end of the day. They couldn't keep it till tomorrow. The girl agreed and paid the money and Julie put the pushchair behind the counter so nobody else got interested. She wrote "deposit paid five euro" on the ticket with the date.

Her reluctance to handle second-hand clothes had long passed. Now she sometimes considered buying things for herself, brand new clothes with the shop labels still dangling, or top quality designer wear. These were few and far between but worth looking out for, and of course as an assistant she got first pick. During a lull in trade a very tall, very black young man took a brown suit into the changing cubicle. He came out and flaunted it.

'You like?' She was honest with him, it fitted well but the wide lapels and the short flared trousers didn't look good. She told him to wait while she went through the men's clothes rack and found a smart navy blue, newer and slimmer, with very long trousers.

'Try this one. Better suit.' He went in and put it on. The shop had quietened for a few minutes, both she and Liz clapped when he came out and did a twirl. It looked excellent.

'For my wedding,' he said proudly, and they congratulated him, 'I am getting married.'

'You will look very smart.' He paid her the five euros and went away pleased as punch. The Moroccan girl was back with her mother in tow, in Spanish she asked for the pushchair. Julie fetched it and wouldn't hand it over until she got her fifteen euros. The girl was adamant that she had said five euros. Julie kept calm and re-iterated that the price was twenty euros and that all she had paid was the deposit. The mother joined in, shrieking at the top of her voice in Arabic, and now all the shop was watching. The girl changed language to English.

'You thief. You take five, I want. You say five.'

'No! I say twenty, you pay five, now you give me fifteen or I keep!' Julie realised that she was speaking pidgin English herself. She clung to the handlebars of the pushchair. The shop was filling up again. Liz could see a battle arising and went to fetch Maggie.

'You thief! I call Police! You give me. I pay five.' Maggie came running. Julie had lost it now and felt like smacking her across the face. Her knuckles were white with hanging on.

'NO! You pay me fifteen or...'

'What's going on?' said Maggie. Julie explained, showing

47

her the ticket.

'Do you want this?' The girl said she did, 'Have you got the fifteen euros?' The girl's mother started to shriek again, 'MADAM, have you got the money?' She gave her the five euros back, 'Thank you,' and they left the shop.

Maggie turned to Julie and whispered, 'Twenty? You must be joking!'

'It's worth a lot more.'

'I'm worth a bloody lot more but I work for nothing. Mark it down to ten.'

The young man who had bought the smart suit came back and saw them writing on the ticket. His eyes lit up.

'How much?' he asked in Spanish. Julie said ten. His face dropped, 'Very beautiful.' he said. Then he told her that he would have bought the pram but now he had bought the suit for his wedding he couldn't afford it. His girlfriend was to have a baby in six months. He got out his money, wrapped in an old envelope, he only had five euros and some change. Nobody was looking, Julie handed him the pushchair, took his five and added five from her own purse, she tapped her nose.

'Our secret,' she said, 'Because you are good customer.' And he went away delighted.

* * * * *

Andrea felt almost a traitor not going to El Marinero for breakfast. She had suggested to Phil that they had a change, went to a different bar.

'I'm fed up with Malc and Mick..' she explained, 'Always going on. It will do us good to go somewhere else.'

They walked along the Paseo hand in hand as they always did. There were so many bars, English, Spanish, you name it. It was a warm sunny day and a lot of people were parading their dogs, doing some shopping, hurrying or just strolling along. They came to a bar called "La Tasca", it looked nice enough so they settled themselves near the front of the terrace and ordered their breakfasts of coffee and cognac.

'I love people watching, don't you?' Phil agreed, though he never took much notice of people or anything else, he was very unobservant. 'Look, there's the twins..' The two identical ladies walked side by side, as though joined at the hip. They were a well known pair in Orilla, dressed in matching clothes, carrying the same shopping bags and walking twin chihuahuas on red leads. 'Oh, it's a real treat not to have to listen to Mick and Malc,' she sighed.

'And Sandra,' he added. Phil found Mick and Malc irritating but Sandra really went too far. He hated the way she showed Mick up in front of everybody. Andrea wasn't perfect but at least she would never do that to him.

'They are alright individually but when they get together..'

'It's the clash of the Titans.' Phil didn't make many funny

remarks, but when he did Andrea always laughed heartily. A man pushing a dirty red moped with a plastic fruit crate bungee-corded to the back steered it round the back of the flower kiosk and went inside. He came out with a blue bucket which he stood inside the fruit crate and then proceeded to tie it on with string. He then filled the bucket half full with water.

'What's he doing?' Andrea wondered, out loud, 'If he takes off on that the water will spill...' He came out of the flower stand carrying so many huge white lilies that his arms could barely reach around them, and plonked them into the bucket. With a quick shuffle to make sure they were all in he mounted the bike and drove off. The scent of lilies poured from him like a jet stream. Andrea breathed it in.

They had finished their coffee in record quick time and there wasn't much left of the brandy.

'That's because we haven't had to listen to the Titans, we've finished already!' said Andrea.

'There's no hurry, we don't have to go yet.' They settled down and watched the people go by. It was strange not having anyone to talk to. Andrea looked Phil up and down. This was the man she had chosen to run off with. It was all like a bad dream, now. She had been so unhappy when Gerald, her husband, had gone off with that tart from Boots the Chemists, and Phil, who had worked in the same office at Amalgamated Construction, had been so kind. It had been a whirlwind romance! Well, that's how she liked to think of it. In reality he wanted to escape the

50

demands of his ex wife Barbara and was looking for an excuse to run. But it had turned out OK, hadn't it?

A woman with an accordion came and stood in front of the terrace.

'Oh, no, the bloody accordion players are back..' said Philip.

'Haven't seen any of them for ages, do you remember the other year? There were thousands of them, queuing up around corners and coming out one after the other. Never seen a woman before, though.' She was middle aged, tidy looking, with huge thick glasses. It was unusual that she was on her own, normally they had an accomplice rattling a tambourine. She started to play. They didn't know the tune but it was jolly and she knew how to play properly, which was also unusual. After the first tune she played another. They thought that was it and were expecting her to pass the hat, but no, she played on. This time she started to sing quietly, they didn't recognise the language but it was probably Romanian. It was a folk song of some kind and she made a fair stab at it. This must be it, they thought, and Andrea opened her purse, looking for small change. She knew Phil wouldn't approve of that, but whispered,

'She is certainly giving us a performance!'

'Don't give them money you'll only encourage them!' Andrea ignored this. Why did he have to be so bloody mean? It was the one side of him she didn't like. The woman played yet another song before she came round, stooping apologetically.

Andrea gave her a whole euro.

'Bon appetit!' she said, which seemed strange, as they had no food on the table.

'Come on, let's get out of here.' said Phil, going towards the bar to pay.

'We could stop somewhere different! Have another coffee, it's only 11.15?'

'Oh, alright.'

After paying they walked further along the Paseo and then found a nice English bar called "Three Dragons". Once again they settled themselves down and when the owner came out they found she was Welsh. They talked to her for a while but she seemed anxious to get back inside. Andrea saw a poster advertising a raffle.

'I'm going to have a go at that! Look, first prize is a wide screen TV, we could do with that, ours has about had it.' She went inside the bar and came out with a single ticket. She put it carefully into the bag that she always wore strung across her body. Phil looked at her disapprovingly. Had she gone mad? The drinks were much dearer here and she had already wasted a euro on that bloody accordion woman.

'Oh, it's such a lovely day. What a shame the weather couldn't stay like this, not get any hotter, this is just perfect.'

A slim, attractive woman in a pencil skirt and flowered

blouse, was pushing the dismantled wire skeleton of a shopping trolley. Onto it she had tied a small amplifier. She parked it in front of them and then went to the pretty gift box strapped on top and produced a CD player and a mike, put on a backing track and started to sing, in English, or something vaguely approaching it. It was the Patsy Cline hit "Crazy". She sang in a strangulated warbling voice that made everybody seated in the bar go quiet and look anxious, worried how long this would go on.

'Crayzeeee, crayzee for beink so lowenly,

Crayzeeee, crayzee for beink so bloooo...'

Like the previous entertainment she was value for money in that she sang four songs, each one of them more tortuous than the last.

'Ladee in rrrred, I am danzing wid yooo, nobody alse, joust yoo an mee...'

A child started to laugh and his mother tried to shut him up. Phil drained his cup, then his brandy.

'Come on, we're off, I can't stand much more of this. She'll want paying next, am I made of money?'

Leaving the Three Dragons they carried on along the Paseo until they neared El Marinero.

'I know!' said Andrea, 'Let's pop into El Marinero, it's been nice seeing other bars but I'd rather get back to our friends.'

Outside the bar there was a large tanker-type vehicle with a huge hose attached. It was a drain clearing machine, colloquially known as a "shit-sucker". The driver was just pulling away. Mick, Malc, Sandra and Jenny all sat outside. Brian was in the doorway.

'Don't come in here,' he shouted to them, 'It stinks.. we've had a blocked toilet, had to get the men out.' Andrea felt cheated, they had missed all the fun. The miasma of sewerage still hung in the air.

'In some bars,' said Sandra, 'they have notices saying do not put paper down the toilet.'

'You will never stop the British dropping toilet paper into the pan. It is part of their culture. No way will they put shitty paper into a waste bin, it's against their religion.' said Malcolm.

'And health and safety,' Mick added.

'Precisely.'

Oh, it's nice to be home, thought Andrea.

Chapter Six

Escape to the Seaside

Pat had been on her own all week. Keith had gone to the UK to do some business and so she had not spoken to a soul, apart from the odd *'Buenas Dias'* and *'Hola'.* It wasn't the week for the quiz and when she had called into the Hospice Shop Julie had been too busy to talk. She decided to go for a walk along the Paseo. She was feeling a bit low, but refused to admit it to herself. 'I am alone, but not lonely..' was a mantra that she often repeated. The thing was that Bob, going like that, had left her strapped for cash. She had had no idea how much it cost to settle up everything, and though they had thought they had a tidy sum put away for emergencies, now it had all gone. She was good at economising and could manage to pay her bills and eat fairly well but there was nothing left for extras.

Pat was a timid kind of person 'Wouldn't say boo..' as Bob used to say. He had handled all the finances, she had never had to worry about banks and credit cards. She had never drawn money from a hole in the wall until now. She didn't drive, either, so the car had had to go. Luckily there was a good bus service in Orilla, though she rarely left the town. Of course the truth was that she was lonely, hadn't any real friends. She couldn't afford to join any of the clubs and societies, that was an expensive game, always going on trips and having parties. Not that she really minded that, the clubs were OK but then they always had a falling out and split down the middle, dividing into two separate factions. And anyway, most of them were couples, she wasn't half of a couple any more.

She sat on a bench in the square and watched a little white pup chasing the pigeons. He was a Westie, a West Highland White. She and Bob had had a Westie once. This one was only a baby, his fur was silky in the sunshine. He stood stock still and stared at the birds, then after a little leap of joy, he lowered his head like a bull at a matador and charged. They flew up like tissues in the wind and settled on the pergola amongst the cerise bougainvillea, and looked down on him. He barked in triumph!

She tried to think what friends she had. There was Roger and Julie, Roger was always interested in her wellbeing, he would ring now and then just to check she was alright, and Julie, too, had a soft side. She knew that some people didn't like Julie, thought she was arrogant and a bit stuck up, but it wasn't true at all. Then there was Keith. And that was that.

She had been here nearly six years now and every year that passed she felt less integrated. The fact was that she couldn't adjust her body clock to Spanish time. She couldn't eat at midnight, or she'd get heartburn, she couldn't stay awake until 5am. She had to get washed and dressed as soon as she got out of bed, and have breakfast before nine. She was ready for lunch at 1pm. Her Spanish neighbours were still in their nightclothes at noon, and only just thinking about breakfast. She was 64 years old and all her life she had had to get up and go to work at 6.30. She still woke at that time most days. Sometimes, if it was dark, she could stretch it out for another hour, but then, that was it, she needed her cup of tea.

When Bob was alive she would get up first and go and make some tea, she would drink a cup on her own then take him one in. That day, that terrible day, she had laid her hand on his shoulder gently, as always, and he was cold. She'd dropped the tea. She knew instantly. The problem was, what to do next. She didn't know how to ring for a doctor, or an ambulance, and anyway her legs had ceased to hold her up, she dropped to her knees and sat kneeling in the hot brown liquid, not feeling the broken china pressed against her flesh. Her whole world stopped at that moment. It had never really started again.

Pat didn't want to keep going over it all in her mind, but sometimes the urge was too strong and it was best to go through it. She remembered that once she had got to her feet she had run downstairs, leaving the door open, and found Elsie and Ivy. They were the only English she knew living in their block. She tapped feebly at the door, then rang the bell. Elsie had taken over, as Elsie would take any situation over. She didn't know what she would have done without them, but they had been too forceful at times. Too overpowering. She never thought of them as friends, though she owed them a lot for helping.

She got up from the bench, she couldn't think about it now, tears were pricking at her eyes. 'I'm alone, but not lonely..' she told herself, but she didn't believe it.

* * * * *

Julie had had to work hard in the Hospice Shop the last couple of weeks because Liz had gone to the UK to see her daughter and

Maribel had been sick. Maribel was a pleasant woman but she always seemed to be letting Maggie down. Apart from that she had done extra days to cover for other people. Now they were all back she and Roger decided to take a break and escape to the seaside. And by that she didn't mean just Orilla del Mar.

Julie booked them in to a Hostel, (a small hotel) in a resort just down the coast called Las Fuentes. Though it wasn't far away they had never been there before and Julie sold it to Roger by telling him that it would be nice and quiet and restful. What she meant by that was it would be very Spanish. She hoped, at last, to get some conversation practice, she certainly hadn't had many meaningful conversations in the Hospice Shop, apart from arguments about prices. Roger went along with it, as he always did. Anything for a quiet life was his philosophy.

Las Fuentes was famous for the fact that fresh water streams ran under the beach and bubbled up in some spots through the fine pebbles. That was all they knew about it. They drove down there and managed to park easily as there was nobody about.

'This is a one-eyed town,' said Roger, 'It's deserted.'

'It's still quite early in the day,' Julie reminded him. They took their bags and walked along a narrow side street to the Hostel Santa Maria. It had been converted from two terraced houses and looked very quaint with its balconies decked with pink geraniums. In the front window was a sign stating "Scandinavian Beds", which seemed strange.

'It's not a brothel, is it?' Roger suggested. Julie laughed,

'I hope not.'

The small reception desk was manned by a Spanish lady with

too much make-up and scarlet hair with black roots. Julie greeted her and told her they had a reservation. She asked for their passports. Now, they both had *Residencia* cards, and normally these were taken in lieu of passports anywhere in Spain. They had used them in Madrid, Barcelona and all places in between. Julie laid them on the counter.

The woman picked them up and scrutinised them under a dim lamp for several minutes.

'These are three years out of date. Finished,' she said in English.

'Well yes, the Government doesn't issue them any more, but I have used them as identification all over Spain.'

'No good. I must have Passports.'

'I haven't brought them, I've never needed to before ....'

'You have a correct *Residencia*, the new type?'

'The paper one, yes, but it doesn't have photos and it says at the bottom that it is not to be used for ID purposes.'

'I look at it.'

'I don't have it here.'

'Then give me passports.' Julie looked at Roger. So much fuss. Roger went for his wallet, he remembered he had copies of the passports in there. He produced them. They were a bit tatty round the edges but.. 'Must be originals.' she insisted. 'There are many bad people about, terrorists. ETA. You know this. I cannot accept these, if the Police find out I will be in big trouble.' Julie in her immaculate blue blouse didn't think she looked much like a terrorist, neither did Roger in a pink M & S polo shirt.

'So? You won't accept our booking?' Roger asked. She sighed.

'I will take copies of your copies but..' she crossed herself, 'If the

Police find out.. I will be in big trouble...' she repeated, then lectured, 'Do not do this again in **any** hotel. This time I will let you stay.' She gave them a small log of wood with a key on a chain at one end. The number 204 was written on a piece of paper sellotaped to the log but this was obscured by a very long length of hairy string wrapped round it. At the end of the string was a credit card sized piece of plastic. Julie stared at this arrangement, 'For the lights.' said the woman and showed them the lift. They went up to the second floor. When they got into the room all was revealed, you had to lock the door from the inside with the key, the string connected the key with the plastic card which went into a slot to turn the electric on. The string reached right across the doorway.

'Bit Heath Robinson,' observed Roger.

After unpacking they took a stroll along the Paseo. There were a couple of shops, a couple of restaurants. A waiter was putting a small table under a tree so that it was half in the shade. A notice board advertised *PAELLA*. The waiter was wrapping the table in a paper cloth, twisting the corners under the legs to keep it in place. It was obvious that that was where the paella would sit when cooked, under the tree so that spiders and leaves could drop into it, not that anybody would bother about that. They marked the spot for a potential lunch later.

Roger suggested they went to the only beach bar for a drink. The beach sloped about 45 degrees down to the sea, and the *chiringuito* was set quite a distance from the pathway. They crunched across the pebbles, their feet sliding on the incline and then anchored two of the chairs at the first table they came across.

'It's so peaceful here, isn't it?' asked Julie, closing her eyes and listening to the choppy sea picking up pebbles and throwing them back, a rhythmic rattling which could lull anyone to sleep. There was no-one else about. The young waitress came out and they ordered drinks, a beer for Roger a *tinto verano* (summer wine) for Julie. 'I've been thinking...' said Julie.

'Careful!' he warned, 'You are supposed to be relaxing, remember?'

'Thinking I might start doing Spanish lessons in September.'

'For who?'

'For whoever wants to come. What do you think?'

'Free?' she nodded,

'I suppose so, hadn't thought that far.'

'If you want to, but I'd have thought you had enough on with the shop.'

'I'll still work at the shop but I'm not covering for all and sundry anymore. One day a week is enough.'

They had forgotten that Las Fuentes was in Granada Province, not Malaga. This meant that with every drink ordered you got *tapas*, free *tapas*. The young girl came out with a plate of something and placed it between them. They both stared. The *tapa* consisted of two cold, fluorescent yellow fish, which, at first glance, seemed to have multiple eyes all over their bodies. On closer inspection it revealed that they had been pickled in some kind of saffron marinade, their skins were wrinkled as though they had been too long in a hot bath, and the 'eyes' were just peppercorns.

61

'I'm not eating that!' said Roger, and Julie picked at it with her fork trying to separate fish from bone, she lifted a tiny morsel to her mouth gingerly.

'It's quite nice...sweet..' Roger was what Julie called "bonephobic". He liked fish but only when it was completely filleted. It seemed to be a "man thing", lots of British men were the same, they had some terror of fish bones in the throat. He agreed to give it a try and delicately teased some of the more substantial flesh off the skeleton, poking it until he thought it was safe. Julie wasn't watching him, she had her eye on a family trudging across the beach towards them, absent-mindedly she speared and ate the very piece of flesh he had been working on for five minutes.

'HEY! That was the bit I had de-boned...' They laughed,
'Sorry...'

The Spanish family consisted of a very fat man, a woman who looked too young to be his wife, a boy kicking a ball and a little girl in a Mickey Mouse top. Then came another woman supporting the arm of an old lady. They headed towards a table two tables down from Roger and Julie. Roger abandoned the fish and, finding a newspaper on a chair, tried to decipher the latest football rumours about La Liga, the Spanish version of the Premier League. Julie continued to pick at the *tapa* and hoped she might be able to eavesdrop. Eavesdropping is something taken for granted in a Country where most people speak English, it can be very entertaining to imagine what gave rise to the snatches of conversation you pick up. When you live in a foreign land you forget what fun eavesdropping can be.

There was a great shuffling of chairs and adjusting of tables until they all got seated. The minute the boy sat down he was up again running around with his ball. The man, one can only assume he was the father, called the waitress over.

'Are your *calamares* authentic?' Julie translated. The girl was puzzled, he explained, 'I mean are they fresh? Do you buy whole fresh squid daily and then cut them up yourselves or are they brought in ready sliced? If they are brought in like that then I don't want them. And I don't want them if they are frozen.' The young girl went to find out. Julie wondered if any English person in a cheap seaside café would ask if the chips were fresh cut or frozen. She doubted it. The girl came back and confirmed that chef, her mother, said they were *'autentico'*. He ordered a ration. He then went on to ask if the *boquerones* were *abierto*. *Boquerones* are fresh anchovies and normally they are served fried whole, the bones are so insignificant that you can eat the lot, tail and all. But he wanted them opened up and boned, a painstaking fiddly task. For the grandmother, he explained, who doesn't have many teeth. This ordering went on some time, with him checking every detail. Meanwhile one of the women produced a mobile phone and rang somebody. She didn't need a phone. You could hear her in Granada.

The little girl, about three, wandered over and stood in front of Roger. She had, around her neck, a whistle on a string. This she proceeded to blow, hard. An ear splitting shriek made them both cringe.

Roger put his fingers in his ears when she blew it again, puckering up her cheeks first so that it was louder. He pulled a funny

63

face, which was fatal. She continued to blow time and time again. They pretended to be amused but it was getting a bit too much. The family did nothing about it, they were still enquiring about the preparation of the food. In the end Roger could stand it no longer.

'Let's pay up and go back to see if the Scandinavian Beds live up to expectations.'

'Not now, I've got a headache!'

'I'm talking sleep. Let's have a siesta before our Paella with the spiders in it. After all the Police will probably raid the joint during the night looking for our passports.'

For all the trouble they had had checking in, the Scandinavian beds were a delight. Gorgeously soft and yet supportive. They both fell deep asleep only to be woken by the roar of motorbikes. Roger sprang off the bed and went to the window. A cavalcade of three hundred bikes was roaring by. It was the annual rally of the Harley Davidson Owners Club. They roared round and round the town, going past their window about twelve times and then settled on the paseo where they parked up for the rest of the afternoon before riding round and round again about 6 o'clock.

Some quiet break this had turned out to be.

* * * * *

In El Marinero the topic of the day concerned integration.

'There is no reason we should integrate more than we want,' said Malcolm. 'It's a fallacy that you must pretend to be Spanish to live

64

here.' Mick agreed with him but didn't want to admit it,

'People should learn the language though.' he maintained.

'**You** don't speak the language,' said Sandra.

'I know a lot of words, woman, I just don't know how to join them up into sentences,' he tried to get back on track, 'Take the Indians in the U.K. They eat curry everyday and wear traditional clothes. Nobody criticises them for it, on the contrary, it's their culture, they are encouraged to preserve their way of life. So why aren't we?'

'You can't call fish and chips and John Smith's bitter **culture!**' said Mick.

'Why not? It's as much a culture as poppadoms and lime pickle, isn't it?'

'Oh, shut up, I could murder a jalfrezi right now,' Sandra remarked, licking her lips and remembering wonderful take-aways from the Indian on the corner of their old street.

'You can get curry here, me and Jenny had a nice meal in the Taj only last Sunday,' said Malcolm.

'Somehow it never seems the same as that curry we used to have on a Friday night, with our feet up in front of the tele...'

'I thought we were talking about integration,' Malc reminded her, 'Some people say they are integrated because they go to one of the festivals, and occasionally eat paella, but to be truly integrated you need to live and breathe Spain and all its works. But how many people do you know like that?' They had to admit, not many.

'If they were that integrated you wouldn't see them in here, though, would you?' suggested Sandra, 'They wouldn't set foot in an English bar.'

They had to admit she had a point.

Chapter Seven

Boy Talk, Girl Talk

One of the first signs of Summer was the arrival of lorries fitted with cranes which lifted little blue and cream houses onto the pavements at strategic points around the town. The kiosks had arrived. They were made of heavy plastic, a cross between a Wendy house and a pagoda. They had moulded roof tiles topped with a fancy acorn finial and moulded cream walls with drop down panels at the front and a door at the rear. Later more lorries would roll up to unload freezers for the ice-cream and finally vans would deliver stacks of bubblegum-pink plastic boxes with see-through sides, pre-loaded with *golosinas*. *Golosinas* was a term that covered all manner of gummy sweets, cola bottles, fried eggs, dentures, prawns, strings of red licorice and tiny hamburgers. These plastic towers were stacked onto the counter of the kiosks, built up like bricks, so that the "kioskee" only had a tiny hole to peer through. When the kioskee was inside the dark little house he or she was barely able to turn round, with packets of *pippas*, nuts and crisps hanging from the ceiling. Despite this the concessions to run kiosks were sort after, the long summer nights would be spent sitting outside on a chair, anyway, so they might as well sit out on a chair and make some money out of it.

Not only the joys of Summer to look forward to this year, 2010, but the football World Cup. Strings of flags of all nations started to adorn the various cafés and bars of Orilla del Mar, large flat screen

67

TV's were purchased and hung on wall brackets. Brian invested in some bunting, even though his philosophy in these early months was not to spend more than he had to, not until the bar was turning a profit. It was all pretty exciting, England had some of the best players in the World, Spain were already European Champions, it was going to be a triumph whichever of the two won. Everyone was hoping for a Spain v England final. Wouldn't that make the cash registers jingle!

* * * * *

Dan lived in one of the newest blocks of flats, and one of the smartest. He had been there just over two years and was one hundred per cent content with his new lifestyle. After his divorce he had come close to a nervous breakdown, his used car business was flourishing but it was killing him, so he sold it off, made a tidy sum, and bought a brand new flat in Orilla del Mar, a place he had never previously visited. He bought "off plan" with a fully fitted kitchen thrown in with the price. Never had he made a better move. He was completely stress free, didn't have to worry about anything, and, surprisingly, wasn't a bit bothered about the fact that he had nothing to do. He wasn't lonely or bored.

Dan was just about to set off one morning to stroll down to Emilio's for some lunch when the doorbell rang. It was the wrong day for his cleaner, Maria, so he was puzzled, and went to open it with a frown on his face. There, in the hall, stood his daughter Lauren, wearing a business suit and holding the extended handle of a small suitcase on wheels. He hadn't seen her for nearly three years. His face lit up.

'Hi, dad.'

'What are you doing here?' he asked as he kissed her on both cheeks, Spanish style.

'Looking up my old dad. I'm on the way to Madrid so I thought I'd take a detour. Well, can I come in?' He stepped aside to let her pass.

Lauren's first impression of the living room was of a very long but not very wide room with a low ceiling from which hung two huge ceiling fans, whirring silently. It was a strange feeling, she thought, like being in a Chinook helicopter that never took off. In the middle of the room stood a solitary single recliner chair facing a large, flat screen, wall mounted TV. Next to it was a black plastic fruit crate (the type you see everywhere in that area) with a tray balanced on top. She was puzzled.

'I thought you'd been here two years..' Dan was proud of his home.

'I have. What do you think? Look, I'll show you around.'

'Where's the furniture?'

'This is it. That chair and the tele, that's all I need.'

'You're joking?' She pointed to the fruit crate, 'Why haven't you got a coffee table?'

'Ah, that, yes, well, I will get one soon.' They went into the kitchen, where the gleaming rows of white units topped with dark blue granite worktops flecked with gold were immaculate. His laptop and printer were set up on the breakfast bar. Lauren opened a cupboard; it was empty. She opened all the cupboards, all empty, no pots, pans, food. All he had in was a packet of tea bags and a bag of sugar held closed with an elastic band. The large silver fridge contained one packet of UHT milk, which, ironically, did not need to be in there. He anticipated her next question.

'I don't buy groceries, no need. I eat out.'

'Every day?' he nodded, 'Every meal?'

'Why not?' She moved towards a door that would indicate a bedroom, inside there was a big double bed without a headboard and another two fruit crates stacked up to serve as a bedside table. This time they were also acting as a bookcase. He wasn't a bit ashamed.

'It's the new me, Lauren! And I like it! I've never been happier. Look, I've got a lovely terrace. The big sliding doors pulled back to reveal a large outside area, but there were no chairs or tables there either, no pot plants, only a washing line and the giant dish of a TV satellite receiver trying to hide around the corner of the L shaped terrace. Newly planted but very green gardens surrounded the block, and the sea could be clearly seen above the rooftops of the old town.

'It's a lovely flat, dad, but why haven't you furnished it? There're no curtains, no rugs. For God's sake you've got the money.' Dan shrugged. She had to admit, he did look well. 'What do you do all day?'

'Nothing... that's the beauty of it. Maria comes in to clean on Tuesdays, puts the washing in the machine when she arrives, hangs it out before she goes and comes back the next day to iron it. I do absolutely nothing. Are you coming to lunch then?'

'I've got a train to catch in Málaga at 5.30..'

'Plenty of time. How's that man of yours, Nigel, isn't it?'

'You know full well he's called Neil.' He opened the door and ushered her through.

'Don't forget to lock up, dad, because if you came back and you'd had a robbery you'd never notice,' she laughed. It was lovely to hear her laugh again.

* * * * *

The customers who came into El Marinero at night were not the same people that came in for the bacon sandwiches in the morning. Occasionally Mick and Sandra might call in for a coffee after they had had a meal in La Abuela but normally the mix was quite different. Two young guys, Dave and Steve, were regulars on the bar stools, talking football with Brian and anybody else who was interested. They were working as painters and usually showed up in paint encrusted boilersuits, straight from work. Big Mac, the diminutive Scotsman and his tall wife, Jean, might put in an appearance and Dan came in most nights for a whiskey and soda. The talk turned to football and the upcoming championship.

'Theo Walcott's not in the team then, not going to South Africa.' said Dave.

'Good, he's a wanker,' said Steve.

'Yes, but he's got pace, we need pace..' replied Dave, lowering his voice as he knew Brian wouldn't tolerate bad language. 'That's right, isn't it, Brian, we need Theo for pace?'

'I'd have picked him, but, I suppose Cappello knows what his plan is.'

'...And Ferdinand's injured, then..'

'Before kick off!' said Dan, joining in, 'How the hell did he manage that?'

'He's always injured..' said Steve, 'You can't rely on these people who have niggling permanent injuries. Mind you, I think he's a wa.....' Dave interrupted him, fast.

'All we need now is for Rooney to get clobbered in the USA game.'

'Or sent off..' said Dan.

'Or sent off,' repeated Brian, 'Trouble is, if Rooney does go down who have we got to take his place?'

'Might be a good thing,' said Dan, 'To relieve the pressure, we rely on Rooney too much.'

'I don't like Rooney,' said Steve,

'That's because you are a City man,' said Dave.

'No, that's not it. I just don't like him.'

'Who DO you like, any of them?' Dan enquired.

'No. They are all a bunch of overpaid fucking wankers!'

'Language!' shouted Brian, 'You can drink elsewhere if you are going to use that kind of language, Steve.'

'Sorry, Brian.' Dan tried to change the subject.

'My daughter paid a flying visit this morning. It was nice to see her. Mind you she did nothing but criticise my furnishings.'

'What, didn't she like what you had chosen, then?'

'No, she didn't like the fact that I haven't got any, well, apart from a chair, a tele and a bed.'

'Sounds alright to me,' said Steve, 'What more do you want?'

'Exactly.'

72

* * * * *

Sandra, Andrea and Lynne sat outside on the terrace of El Marinero. The bacon sandwiches had been consumed and Lynne hoped she had finished cooking for the day. Lynne had come to hate cooking. All three women were sick of the football already and had left the "boys" to chew over the USA v England game which had been declared "so-so" except for the appalling error of the English goalkeeper, who had fumbled the ball and let it go over the line.

They sat watching the world walk by.

'You don't see many of those dogs now, do you?' asked Sandra.

'What dogs?' said Lynne.

'You used to see a lot of funny looking dogs, they had their bottom teeth sticking out over their top lip,' she pulled a face to illustrate what she meant, 'And they had squashed faces and heads too big for their bodies. Years of in breeding I suppose. Now all you see are French Bull Terriers and other, fancy, pedigree breeds.'

'You're right, I remember those dogs,' said Andrea, 'Little dogs, flea bitten.'

'That's it. Did I tell you the story of the dog I saw in the mountains?' Andrea had heard this story, many, many times, but as Lynne hadn't she didn't say anything. Sandra went on. 'We went for a ride up the mountains, I think it was when we got the four wheel drive, Mick wanted to test it out. Anyway we drove up higher and higher and got to the point where we had actually gone over the summit. Hadn't seen another car for an hour or so and we were so very high up. We

73

pulled into a lay-by, got out to look at the view and noticed that there was a strange looking house down a long drive. Up there, all on its own. It had big gates and it looked run down, the sort of place you'd get in a horror film. Creepy, even in broad daylight. Then this small dog ran up the drive towards us, barking, and I swear, on my life, that it had a human face.' Lynne thought she was joking and was waiting for the punch line, but she was deadly serious. 'Mick denies it but I'm telling you he went as white as a sheet and was back in the car before I was. It was the scariest thing I've ever seen.'

The three women said nothing, mulling this over. They continued to people watch.

'You can tell the Germans from the English..' said Lynne, changing the topic from dogs to clothes.

'How?' asked Andrea, 'They look the same to me.'

'Their clothes fit. When they buy them they have them altered if they don't. The English wear them straight off the peg, too tight, too loose, whatever.' They reflected on this and decided it was true. Lynne, who was always immaculately turned out couldn't understand how Sandra could look at herself in the mirror at all. Her limp wavy hair had been home-dyed a yellowish blonde, but the underlying grey was clearly visible. She wore a shapeless T shirt with writing which made no grammatical sense, having been chosen by a Chinese designer who couldn't read it, and washed out denim *piratas* (calf length trousers) with shocking pink crocs. But her nails were manicured with bright pink varnish, and her hands were completely blemish free with long, elegant fingers. From the wrists up, though, Lynne thought, she looked a mess. And as for Andrea....

74

At that point they were surprised to see Pat approaching, wearing a big smile and clutching a plastic bag as though it contained something precious. They welcomed her and Lynne went inside to fetch her the tea she asked for.

'I've been to see Julie in the Shop..' she said, opening the bag to let them look inside, 'She saved me this lovely dress, it fits a treat..' They inspected it, a royal blue linen dress with short sleeves, 'She put it by for me.' They all admitted that that was good of her. 'Actually I was hoping that they might have some underwear, my bras are falling to bits.'

Andrea was appalled, 'You wouldn't wear second-hand undies..'

'I just don't know where to get them from..'

'The market,' said Sandra, 'There's this gypsy woman, she has loads of them for two euros each..' Pat knew the woman's stall, she was an expert on the market by now.

'Yes, but they are all funny sizes, I can't work out which size I want.'

'No problem! She stands back and weighs you up then she takes her hands, like this..' she held up both hands in a claw like fashion, 'And she cups your breasts and says 110 Double D or whatever. She's never wrong.' Pat didn't fancy this procedure, and she didn't think the woman would have big enough hands as she was rather well endowed.

'I get mine from CC..' said Andrea, 'Dunnes at CC.' CC was short for *Centro Commercial* which was their nearest shopping mall. Lynne came back with the tea for Pat. 'Pat's looking for new undies. I told her to go to the CC..'

'Bob and I used to go all the time.' Pat recalled, 'Can you get a bus there?'

'I'm sure you can..' said Sandra, 'From the bus station.'

'I think I'll go next week. Make a day of it.'

'You'll need lots of knickers and bras when it gets hot,' Sandra advised Lynne.

'**When** it gets hot...isn't it hot now?' asked Lynne, startled by this comment. They all shook their heads.

'Nowhere near as hot as it will be in August.' Lynne couldn't bear the thought of that, she couldn't sleep now, the fan they had on a floor stand just moved the air around, it didn't cool it. Last night she had dragged a mattress onto the terrace and slept there, but they were too near the road and mopeds would scream past in the early hours of the morning. When she got up she felt as though she had been run over by one of them.

A family came and settled itself around the next table, Lynne swung into waitress mode. Andrea whispered to the others.

'Didn't they do any research before they bought this bar? Surely they realised how hot it gets in Summer?'

'It's one thing thinking you know how hot it gets, another entirely when you experience it.' said Sandra, 'Pat, did I ever tell you about the dog I saw in the mountains?' Andrea got up to find Phil, she couldn't listen to that again.

Chapter Eight

Driving Forces

Pat was so relieved that she had chosen to go to the CC on the bus instead of accepting the lift offered by Elsie. Elsie and her sister Ivy had been a Godsend after Bob died but she couldn't face another trip in their beaten up old car, it frightened the life out of her.

Elsie was 83 and still driving. She drove like Lewis Hamilton on crack. Ivy, her sister cowered in the back, having read somewhere that it was the front seat passenger who always came off worse in a crash. Elsie swore at other motorists, cut them up, ignored road signs and hated the *Guardia* with a passion. Amazingly the *Guardia* had never stopped her once, which was probably a good thing as she had an expired UK Driving Licence and very poor eyesight.

Pat was watching the other passengers. There was an old man sitting next to her who had rolled his bus ticket into the shape of a cigarette and put it gently between his lips. He was going all the way to Malaga, and it would probably stay there until he arrived. Across the aisle a Senegalese man held a pair of sunglasses in his hand and squinted into the sunlight. He had taken them from his stock in case he was forced to wear them, but was putting off the actual moment when he placed them on his nose. This, Pat reckoned, was because they still had the label attached and he intended to put them back into stock when he returned.

She was wearing her new blue dress and it looked a treat. She

77

had washed and ironed it especially and added some chunky beads ready for the outing. I must do this more often, she told herself. She spent a pleasant morning walking around the shops and finally went to Dunnes where she bought two bras, trying them on to make sure they fitted. She also got a pack of knickers, which were reduced in price, so she was quite pleased with herself and decided to go to the coffee shop, the one that she and Bob always used to visit. There were no empty tables and she hesitated, wondering whether to stay or not when a voice said,

'You can sit here, if you want.' An elderly lady with snow white hair was indicating an empty chair. Pat thought she looked harmless and so she joined her.

'They only gave me three weeks to live,' was the first thing the woman said.

'Really? When was that?'

'Two and a half years ago. The other Specialist said they should never do that, you can't tell, it could be three weeks, three years or longer. He was very annoyed about it.'

'You look well enough..' Pat decided, and then the waiter came over for her order. For a change she ordered a *naranja natural,* she knew the freshly squeezed orange juice would be more expensive than coffee but, what the hell, this was a special treat.

'Course, I was in the hospital then. Don't let them send you there! Don't get me wrong, they are wonderful medically speaking, no expense spared, every drug and procedure, but bedside manner, don't know the meaning. Treat you like a car on a ramp, clinical, never ask you if you feel OK, just insert probes and give you injections in the middle of the night. Come round at midnight asking if you want coffee! I ask you, wake you up for that. That is, if you can sleep. Two bedded rooms, the other person with their entire extended family camping out in shifts, literally camping out, with camp beds and thermos flasks, talking at the tops of their voices, watching TV till 2am with the fluorescent lights on, and the food, diabolical, it is, boiled fish and no seasoning. Then they put me in a home,' said the woman, 'My son, he said, I've got the business, mum, I can't look after you, unless you want to move back, I said I should cocoa, I'm not going back there, that would finish me off, so he had to put me in a home. It was terrible! Don't let them ever put you in a home. Cost the earth, too. Nobody spoke English, patients or staff, nice room but no English TV only Spanish and you know what drivel that is, even if you speak the lingo, but the worse thing was the food, or rather the lack of it, they didn't feed me it was awful.'

'Didn't feed you?'

'Only those pea things, you know, beans in broth and soup like the bottom of a water butt with things floating in it. No meat, no fish, only lentils and gruel. My Specialist he said to me you're losing weight. I said well I have got cancer he said no that's not it you are anaemic and I said well can you doubt it I don't get any protein, no meat, no fish and no fresh vegetables,' The orange juice was set in front of Pat but she barely noticed, the woman's story was so compelling. She spoke ten to the dozen, hardly stopping to breathe, 'Then he said how about trying an experimental drug I said I'll try anything, I was in a lot of pain then, and he gave me one pill a day, just a little pill within two days I felt ten years younger. The magic bullet I call it, anyway I said to my son you have got to get me out of here, I am going stir crazy and so he got me a little flat just up the road from here. Now I can cook my own dinners again and I have steak and roast beef and Yorkshire, I don't mind that I'm cooking for one! Tonight I've got salmon steaks new potatoes and spinach, that's what you call nutrition. Are you a widow?'

'Yes, my Bob died last year, in his sleep.'

'Ten years since Fred went. Can I give you some advice?'

'Please do...' she leaned forward and grasped Pat's hands in hers, squeezing hard.

'If you get a chance to have a new man, grab it with both hands. I had the chance and I let him go.'

'There is someone I'm fond of...' Pat admitted, a picture of Keith coming into her mind.

'There you go. Don't wait until you think the time is right. Go for it, girl!'

Pat only wished she had this woman's courage.

* * * * *

When he set up the quiz Mick knew that it would be while the World Cup was on. He didn't want to make it too football based, but felt he had to include some element of the competition to make it topical. He decided to do a picture round based on the flags of the countries that had qualified, unfortunately the local free ex-pat magazine, "The Farola" had published a couple of pages with a similar theme and Mick hadn't read the new edition as he had been too busy compiling his questions. He didn't believe in buying them off the Internet, like most people did, he carefully constructed each one and then cross checked it with Google. It took him hours. On the night of the quiz most people sat outside on the terrace. It was so pleasant after the heat of the day to be sitting in the almost fresh air. Exhaust fumes from cars backing up and trying to find a parking space added to the smell of meat barbecuing in La Abuela's overpowered the faint whiff of jasmine growing up an old tree on the Paseo, but it was still a lovely evening.

As soon as Mick gave out the Picture Round there was a flurry of excitement he couldn't understand. The latest copy of The Farola had been delivered to El Marinero that morning and everybody had picked one up when they arrived before the quiz and thumbed through it. Now they were surreptitiously trying to read it under the tables. Those who hadn't got a copy soon caught on and went into the bar to see if there were any left. The only person who hadn't worked it out was Mick himself. Roger said to Julie,

'Do you think I should say something? They are all cheating..'

'No, keep out of it,' said Julie, 'Is that Algeria?' Pat looked under the table,

'Yes..' she whispered. 'Shouldn't we put a few wrong? Won't it be suspicious?'

'I could mix a couple of them up? So it's not too obvious,' Julie suggested.

'Bet the others won't bother. Fill most of them in and we'll guess the rest,' Roger decided.

When it came to checking them at the end of the quiz nearly every team had them all right, except Roger and Julie who had two the wrong way round.

81

'I don't get it!' said Mick, 'There's something funny going on here, I smell cheating.'

'Don't be ridiculous,' said Sandra, 'You are paranoid you are. You just don't get how interested everybody is in the World Cup.' Mick wasn't convinced, it wasn't until they got home and he had a brief look at the magazine that he realised what had happened. He went ballistic. Sandra thought it was the funniest thing that had happened for ages.

* * * * *

Lynne had lost her driving force. That was the trouble, she decided. She had always led the way when it came to decisions, wasn't this why they had come? Because **she** wanted a fresh start. She didn't feel it was going quite to plan. The heat was sapping her energy, she couldn't sleep and she couldn't think. She seemed to spend her whole life locked up in that tiny kitchen, the smell of bacon had impregnated her skin, no amount of Chanel No 5 could mask it. The customers weren't quite what she had expected, either, she thought them all strange. But the most alarming thing of all was that Brian seemed to be getting on so well with them, he almost seemed to be enjoying it. If anybody was to throw in the towel early she'd thought he would. He didn't mind the long hours, but then he was used to that, that was the reason that they had become so detached from each other, his job and her job travelling all over the country, staying in four star hotels. How she had complained about those hotels, and now she would just love to stay a few nights in that air conditioned, mini-barred heaven. Instead of sleeping on the terrace eaten by mosquitoes, or tossing and turning on top of the sweaty sheets.

'Seize the day!' she told herself, 'Pull yourself together woman and take charge. Get out of the kitchen and look at El Marinero in a new light. What can you do to make it look more inviting? It looks like every other bar on the Costa, with advertisements for English breakfast and the times of football matches on a board outside. That day she had an appointment at the hairdresser's. Thank God she had found a good hairdresser. Pauline, a girl from London, was a brilliant stylist, very artistic with lots of new ideas. Very cutting edge without resorting to the kind of haircuts that made middle aged women like Lynne look like silly girls, or, on the other hand, like little old ladies. She had every confidence in Pauline, and it was while she was at the backwash having aloe vera shampoo massaged into her hair that the idea came to her. A flash of genius, she thought, and she couldn't wait to tell Brian all about it.

She had pre-warned the regulars that there wouldn't be any cooking until after 11am. When she got to El Marinero Mick and Malc were in the middle of that day's debate.

'The trouble with the Spanish is that they have no gene of forethought.' said Mick, thinking the concept one of his more impressive statements.

'How do you mean?' asked Malcolm.

'Well, for example, if you had a dog you would lock the gate because you would see that he could get out on the road and be run over. It probably wouldn't enter their minds, the dog would get out, cause an accident and there would be a lot of wailing and "act of God"

83

stuff. You see, no gene of forethought.' Sandra got it, at least,

'Like when they chose market day to tarmac the main road? The one day that the traffic doubles because of the diversion?'

'Exactly. They never think ahead.'

'Last Summer when nobody could park anywhere, they decided to re-paint the yellow lines. In some places they stopped one side of a parked car and continued the other, finishing up with dotted lines!' said Malcolm, catching on, wishing he'd thought of it first.

'Precisely.' Mick folded his arms in self satisfaction. He'd got them this time.

'And they leave the abandoned cars for years and then put removal notices on them in August...why can't they shift them before the tourists arrive?' said Phil.

Lynne went inside where Brian was unpacking some stock.

'I've been trying to get hold of Geoff,' he said, 'That freezer is on the blink, the one you keep your bacon and stuff in, and I can't find a guarantee or anything.'

Lynne ignored this, she also ignored the fact that he hadn't said a word about her hairdo. She just couldn't wait to tell him what she had decided.

'I've had an idea..'

'Not now, love, we have to get hold of Geoff, this is important, if that freezer conks out then we'll lose all our stock.' He pushed past her and went out onto the terrace. 'Anybody know why I can't get hold of Geoff?'

'Didn't you know?' asked Andrea, 'He's done a runner.'

'What?'

'Done a runner. A midnight flit. Geoff and Dagmar have disappeared leaving a trail of unpaid bills behind them.'

'That's brilliant, that is, anybody know of a freezer repair man?' They discussed it, somebody said Paco Fridge Man used to be OK, somebody else thought he had retired.

'Brian,' said Lynne, 'I need to talk to you...'

'Not now, Lynne, later.'

'Lynne, can we have our bacon sandwiches, now, we're starving,' said Malc. Lynne stomped off into the kitchen.

She didn't get to talk to Brian until he came home that night. Lynne had been in bed for hours, but couldn't sleep. It was about 2.30am and he was completely worn out. He sat on the edge of the bed to take his sandals off when she sat bolt upright and made him jump.

'Thought you were asleep! I've got a man out to look at the freezer, he's coming tomorrow he...'

'You know that blank piece of wall outside on the right of the doors?'

'Yes, what about it?'

'I've asked Pauline, she's very artistic you know, to paint me a full size figure of a sailor, you know "El Marinero" and then her boyfriend, Manolo, is going to fret cut it out of hardboard. It will have a space we can write things on, like "Quiz Tonight" that kind of thing and will be turning towards the entrance, to welcome people in. I think it will be so impressive. Something different, make us stand out from the rest.' Brian was too tired to discuss this. His first thought was that it was a daft idea, but he hadn't the energy to argue.

'What'll it cost?'

'Oh, I knew you'd say that! That's all you ever think about.' She got out of bed and dragged the single mattress onto the terrace. 'GOOD NIGHT'. She screamed.

* * * * *

'Did you see the football? The Algeria game?' asked Roger, getting himself seated at the bar, next to Steve who knocked off work early on a Friday.

'Wish I hadn't,' said Brian, 'What an absolute disgrace.'

'I'll have a *sin alcohol,* a *zero-zero*, please, Brian. Got to go and pick Julie up in a minute.' Brian poured some of the beer into a glass and gave him the rest in the bottle. 'So boring, wasn't it? At times there seemed twice as many men in green as men in white.'

'Why didn't he play Joe Cole?' asked Steve.

'God knows. And why Heskey? Heskey and no Crouch. You've got little Defoe running about all over the place, he couldn't get to those headers like Crouch...'

'I don't like Heskey,' said Steve.

'And then there's Sean Wright-Phillips, he's fast but..' added Brian.

'I don't like him. Didn't like his dad.'

'You don't like any of them!' said Roger.

'No, they're all a bunch of f....'

86

'Watch it!' said Brian, quickly 'I've warned you before.' Steve got down from the stool and pushed some coins across the bar, with a wry smile he left.

'Went for my ITV today,' said Roger, referring to the Spanish version of the MOT, not the British television station.

'How did it go?'

'Oh, it passed, but I hate the system there, I hate it.'

'What happens then?'

'Well, you have to book in in advance, then you show up and wait for them to call out your registration number. Problem is that the loudspeaker is SO loud and ancient that you can't understand what they say..some old boy had to tell me they were reading out my number. Then you drive down the line while they check the car. At one point they go underneath in a pit and they give you a microphone. Next time I'm taking Julie, though I doubt even she would understand it.' He took a draught of his beer, 'Funny thing is, that, afterwards, when you get to the petrol station about half a mile away you can hear the loudspeaker as clear as anything. No probs..'

'Glad I haven't got a car here, I don't need one, I never get a day off.'

'You'll be glad you've no car when the hordes come down, it's bad enough now but in August you might as well hibernate. We're going to the UK on Saturday for six weeks.'

'So is Malcolm.'

'There won't be many Brits here, I can tell you. They get away if they can.'

87

Lynne was eagerly awaiting the delivery of her sailor figure. Manolo had promised to drop it round on his motorbike that morning on his way to work. She was sitting outside, even before Andrea and Phil had turned up, and as promised the young man arrived with a six foot high brown paper parcel precariously tied to the back of the bike. She ran over and paid him without stopping to look and then lay it down across two tables to undo the packing. Brian came to watch. He knew she was excited about this but wasn't at all sure about it himself. He just hoped she would be pleased with the finished product.

'I just hope you are not disappointed,' he commented. The trouble was that Pauline was more used to painting fashion models, young girls with trendy outfits, models' faces with flowing locks, she had never attempted to paint a man before. And it showed. 'He looks a bit ...well... feminine, doesn't he?'

El Marinero had a slender frame, tiny waist, delicate hands and a dainty look. Lynne didn't say a word. She thought the same herself, but decided it would be OK once he was upright and she lifted the figure and propped it against the wall where she had intended it to go, stepping back and hoping for an improvement.

'It's bloody awful. You're not putting that up!' said Brian, 'We'll be a laughing stock.' At that point Andrea and Phil, Mick and Sandra all arrived together. Mick took one look and effecting a camp posture cried,

'Oh, hello sailor!' They all fell about laughing. Lynne ignored them.

'I want it putting up, get your drill, Brian.'

'No. Sorry Lynne but he'll have to go back for a re-paint before I put that outside.'

'They'll think it's a gay bar..' suggested Phil, 'Perhaps you should open a gay bar, I hear they make good money..' Lynne stomped off and hid in the kitchen, telling them,

'And you needn't think you'll be getting bacon sandwiches, I'm on strike.'

The jokes continued, even in the kitchen she could still hear them laughing. The most annoying part was that they were right, the whole thing was a fiasco. She just hoped that Brian wouldn't find out what she had paid for it. What did she do now? She couldn't put it up, she couldn't ask Pauline to alter it, Pauline had done her best, it wasn't her fault she could only paint women.

She heard Malcolm and Jenny arrive, Malcolm had a deep guffawing sort of laugh, she'd know it anywhere. At that point she knew that she hated these stupid people. She took a deep breath and marched outside, picked up the sailor figure, crossed the road, stopping the traffic as she did so, stamped on it till it broke in half and threw it into the giant wheelie bin. As she marched back past the open mouthed stares of her regulars she cried out so everybody even the Chinese next door could hear her,

'Happy now?' and went and hid in the toilet.

Chapter Nine

Reasons to be cheerful

"The Very Noble, Royal and Most Excellent Town Hall of the Ancient Villa of Orilla del Mar" as it described itself on its letterheads, or "they" as the ex-pats called it, was one of the few town halls not to have had its Mayor and half its council locked up in gaol. All along the coast Mayors had been arrested for crimes concerning bribery and corruption, acceptance of monies in exchange for building permits and other doubtful dealings. The present economic climate had resulted in a tightening of authority belts, some cuts in services such as street cleaning, and the cancelling of projects such as a much needed football pitch, the provision of social housing and repairs to the Paseo. However the council had not abandoned what it considered to be its most prestigious and vital project, the Interpretation Centre of the *Almejitas Blancas,* a rare, near extinct tiny white shellfish with a split lentil sized piece of flesh which could now only be found in one or two of the rocky bays just outside of their town. The rest of Spain had fished it out years ago as it was considered a delicacy, scouring the sea bed until it was devoid of all life. The Town Council was sure that the three hundred thousand euros project, where people could learn about this boring greyish little clam, looking at diagrams and a few live samples in dimly lit tanks, would bring in tourists by the bus load. It also, like every other Town Council in Spain, would never, ever, in a month of holy Sundays, tamper with the size and traditions of the annual Féria.

Every village, town and all the big cities had their own Féria, usually celebrated around the date of the Patron Saint of the town. They ranged from two day affairs set up in a dry river bed to two week extravaganzas in the big cities. The Féria of Orilla del Mar was quite a substantial one for the size of the town, it had a dozen or so *casetas*, which were open air pubs with canvas sides, some serving *tapas* or just drinks by the litre (a jug full of a *combinado*, like whiskey and coke or gin and tonic, to be shared amongst friends). Some put down wooden floors for a bit of dancing and had music blaring out into the night air. There were open air food stalls selling *churros* (a breakfast doughnut usually served with cups of thick dunking chocolate), roast chickens on spits and pieces of coconut cooled by running water. There were lots of market type stalls and hot dog stands and simple games like hook a duck or hit a dartboard. In the middle of the Féria was the main music venue, where twin stages faced each other so that two orchestras or bands could set up to play alternately, and with a large concrete dance floor in the centre. Here there would be several headline acts, with flamenco displays and famous singers. On top of this there was a fun fair with the usual attractions, dodgems, inflatable bouncy Homer Simpsons, roundabouts and fairly tame "dare devil" rides like the Crazy Frog and Rodeo Bull.

Of course there had to be a religious aspect and on the last night the statue of the Virgin on a heavy platform decorated with fresh white flowers was paraded on the shoulders of men dressed in sailor suits, who walked barefoot across the beach and loaded her aboard a waiting boat lit by candles. This then sailed along the sea's edge to the

91

accompaniment of a huge firework display set off with little regard for health and safety by a man on the beach. All this on top of a week of competitions for all ages, fishing, dominoes, sack races, and children's entertainments.

* * * * *

'Of course you do realise,' said Mick as a subdued Lynne served his breakfast to him outside on the terrace, 'That this bar won't be able to operate as per usual during the Féria.' This was news to Lynne.

'How do you mean?'

'Well, for a start off you'll have to order in some portable bar units.'

'What are they?' Sandra explained.

'All the bars along here barricade themselves in with portable fridge counters, with beer pumps on top and barrels underneath. They bring everything outside and make a barrier across the front. No serving at tables, customers have to come to the bar and get served.' Lynne called Brian outside to hear all this, Mick was quite happy to repeat it.

'But why? Why not let them inside?' Brian asked.

'Do you want 5,000 people using your toilet? Because that's what's going to happen if you leave the bar open,' he warned.

'You're joking!' said Lynne.

'No, he's not..' added Andrea, 'Is he Phillip?'

'There are no public toilets and all the bars stop people going in, unless they know them. Even though under Spanish law they are entitled to use them. Last year they reckon there were six thousand

92

people here on the Sunday night alone.' Phillip confirmed.

'You can make a small fortune if you want to,' Mick continued, 'But you'll have to be prepared to stay open all night, till around 7am at least.'

'Last year,' said Andrea, 'We could still hear the disco music at 9 am in our flat'

Lynne didn't like this talk of fortunes. She was sure that Brian would expect her to stay up all night just to make a few bob.

'Actually,' said Phillip, 'You've probably left it too late to get your bar units now, and also, you'd have to get some help, two of you wouldn't cope.' Lynne was relieved to hear this, thank you Phil, she told herself.

'Why didn't you tell us before?' asked Brian, annoyed.

'We thought Geoff would have filled you in?'

'Geoff! Don't talk to me about Geoff. I'd like to fill him in. I'm still getting people rolling up that he owes money to.'

'The other option,' said the man they called Wikipedia, 'Is to open all day and then close and lock everything inside at night.'

'That suits me!' said Lynne, looking at Brian, 'I don't think we've any other option, it's a pity, but we've left it too late.'

'I'll have a go at getting the bar units, look into it...but..perhaps Lynne's right.'

'You won't get any sleep at home,' said Sandra, 'Too much noise, so you might as well be working.' Lynne gave her a piercing stare, 'Whose side are you on?' she thought.

* * * * *

93

England were out of the World Cup. Knocked out by Germany, their old foe. The general consensus of opinion was that they had been an embarrassment. The usual football pundits gathered the night before the Féria to discuss what had been a diabolical game.

'England were a disgrace,' said Steve.

'Don't mention it, it makes me feel sick.' Dave added.

'Absolute disgrace,' Brian repeated. 'Where was the defence?'

'God knows. It was like watching kids play in the park.'

'No, worse than that. Kids in the park look like they are enjoying it. They run at people, they tackle...' Brian surmised.

'...they take chances..' added Steve. 'And where was Rooney? He didn't show up. He sent a lookalike I think.'

'It's the biggest disaster since Beckham got himself sent off that time..'

'Beckham got death threats.'

'So will Rooney.' They all took a slurp of their beer, simultaneously. The sighs were audible as they set their glasses down, 'Spain will win I think. Not that they've been anything to write home about. None of them have, come to that.'

'I blame Cappello, I don't like Cappello,' said Steve.

Brian took a pair of scissors and ceremoniously cut the flag of St George from the string of flags that hung round the bar. He tied the two ends together uniting Brazil with North Korea. They could have cried, to a man they were sick as parrots.

* * * * *

94

The first time that Pat and Bob went to the Féria they were so impressed. The wonderful display of multicoloured lights strung from side to side all down the Paseo, the huge "gate" of lights at the entrance, the fireworks, it was all so exciting. But as the years passed they found it all a bit "samey". The noise started to annoy them, they couldn't sleep and yet they couldn't stay awake long enough to go and see "The Four Tenors" or whoever else was top of the bill because they didn't start until 1am. Fighting their way through the crowds for a glimpse of a doll like statue on a platform lost its appeal. Like the religious processions of Easter, once you'd seen one, you'd seen them all. Ornaments on sticks, Bob used to call them. This year she stayed away completely. She had no compunction to wander alone between Spanish families having such a good time, surrounded by all their friends. Pat had to admit that she liked to see the little girls dressed in miniature Flamenco costumes, even tiny babies in prams had their *vestidos de volantes,* dresses of frills and polka dots arranged around them so they appeared to be sitting in the middle of a flower, their tiny heads adorned with a comb and a rose, little spotted shoes with heels on their feet. Sometimes the mothers would be dressed to match which looked so impressive. But this year she stayed in, put the air conditioning on and watched the TV. Shutting herself away from all the action, longing for it to be over. It was only three days after all.

* * * * *

If Andrea and Phil had had the money, that is if Phil would part with the money, they would have taken a plane and got out of there.

You couldn't park, so you couldn't go anywhere. Their flat wasn't too near the centre of the action but they could still hear it with all the windows closed. They went down and had a walk around in the early part of the evening, about 10.30, trying to get in the mood but nothing kicked off till midnight. Sometimes, thought Andrea, I wonder what I am doing here surrounded by foreigners. How did I come to be in the middle of something I could never feel part of? She could see there was an attraction, and originally she had tried very hard to enjoy it, but the cacophony of sound, the pushing and shoving of crowds, the screaming of babies who should be in bed and the smells of hot dogs and candy floss, fried fish and chocolate turned her stomach.

* * * * *

Lynne had got her way, it was far too late to get bar counters, far too late to get staff. They opened for breakfast as usual and did quite well with the people who had been up all night. Spanish people on holiday always breakfast out, and though El Marinero would not normally be their first choice, as most other breakfast cafés were closed they came to them. Some toast, jam and butter or oil and tomato was much easier to prepare than the full English, though she had to admit that they made a terrible mess on the table, it took her much longer to wipe down. She struggled a bit with the twelve different strengths of coffee but Pepe the Coffee Man had left her a chart and she wrote numbers on this and showed it to the customers. They made more money from breakfasts than they usually took at night, so Brian was happy. They locked everything up and went home at nine. It was the first time they had had any time together, they felt awkward sitting on the hard settee watching Spanish television.

On the Sunday morning as the cleaning people were hosing down the pavements one of their first breakfast customers was Paco Car Hire. Everybody called him Paco Car Hire to distinguish him from Paco Fridge Repair, Paco Sardines and Paco Bread Van. He was an infrequent customer of theirs but as he spoke near perfect English they always welcomed him. He was an expert in "The Spanish Way" as he called it, and they would consult him about the whys and hows of various local customs.

'My God!' he said, 'You are open!'

'Yes, we decided to do days and not nights.'

'Very sensible. You would not like to be up all night, it is very hard work.'

'Tell me,' said Brian, 'Do they get any trouble at night?'

'How do you mean?'

'Well, like fights, that sort of thing, drunken behaviour.'

'Oh, no. It is not the Spanish way...'

'But surely sometimes..'

'Maybe. But not like England. When I was in Brighton, I worked there for ten years, we had many problems with drunk people. The Police, they were always coming round. I was a young man then, I had never seen anything like it.'

'You should see it now, Paco, the women are the worst. They go out with hardly any clothes on, even in Winter, they look like tarts, and they get legless, fall over, vomit and wet themselves. And they fight, tear each others hair out.' Paco sniffed at this idea.

97

'That is not good.' Lynne brought him his coffee and toasted roll.

'Tell me,' said Brian who had had one or two fleeting visits from Trish, the mystery woman, 'Who is the woman that lives in your flat?'

'Ah, that is Treesh,' he said, pronouncing it in a drawn out way, 'Treesh is very good girl.' Brian thought "girl" was a bit of misnomer, 'She has been on top of me for many years.' Brian smothered a laugh, 'She came to me one day, oh, about fifteen years now, and she say she wants to drive to Marbella...I said lady,. Do not go there on your own, very bad people there, criminals, and very expensive. You rent my flat and stay here in Orilla del Mar, and she has been there ever since. She was an entertainer, you know.'

'Really?' said Lynne, taking an interest now.

'Oh yes. She knows many famous people. She knows them very well. Treesh is a very good girl, I don't think she has much money, she lives a simple life. I like that, simple life.'

'Does she have a boyfriend, a man?'

'No. She needs no man. She is a free spirit.'

Brian had heard otherwise.

* * * * *

For Trish the Féria was the best time of the year. Every night she would sleep until midnight, put on her best black jeans and flip flops with diamonds between the toes, plaster on the eye makeup and the purplish pink lipstick and go out on the prowl. Tonight, she decided to put on a diamond bracelet as a special touch. The average person, looking her up and down, would never dream that the slim silver bangle

98

with the large stones was anything but lookey-lookey man trash, but in fact the diamonds were real. Her twenty-first birthday present from Daddy. She finished the outfit with a small black beaded bag on a shoestring strap slung across her body into which she could just squeeze her cigarettes, lighter, a lipstick, some money and a spare thong.

She lived entirely on *tapas* in order to maintain her skinny look. She hadn't had a proper meal in years. So the Féria, with its dearth of *tapas* eating possibilities was a positive gala feast for her. After whetting her thirst with a Cuba Libre in the first *caseta* she ordered a *tapa* of thinly sliced Serrano ham. She ate delicately and slowly, chewing each morsel several times. She sat alone at a table amongst tables overloaded with plates and glasses and surrounded with gangs of friends or family groups. One by one they came and took the other three chairs until she was sitting at a table for one. After she had finished her drink she got up and walked around the fairground, watching the people screaming on the rides and the toddlers bouncing on the inflatables. She then moved on to another *tapas* bar where she consumed cheese, cut into thin wedges, and then to another where, with her third Cuba Libre of the night she indulged in *gambas.*

Trish took eating *tapas* very seriously. She carefully beheaded each prawn, cracked open its starched pink jacket, pinched off its legs with her purple painted talons, and tore off its tail. All that remained was a tiny maggot of salty pink flesh. She chewed it carefully. By this time she was ready for a smoke and went to sit on a bench near the beach. All around her people were buzzing, the music throbbed in the disco bars, the screams could be heard from the Rodeo Bulls and the

99

sweet sickly smell of candy floss and waffles permeated the warm night air. She lit one of her dark tobacco cigarettes. A large man came and sat at the other end of the bench. He eyed her up and down. He was a big man, strong and full bodied was how she saw him. Anybody else would have thought him fat. He had fair hair thinning in front and wore frameless glasses. When he turned his head she saw he had a rat's tail of hair held with an elastic band. Even this did not put her off. He didn't look Spanish. He took out cigarettes and asked her for a light, she obliged.

'Are you English?' he asked, in a foreign accent of some sort.

'Yes, darling, 'fraid I am..'

'I am from Germany, from Frankfurt. I am here two weeks..in an apartment of my brother..'

'Having a good time, darling?' He said he was enjoying the fiesta. 'I live here,' she said, 'I love Orilla.' Then she thought she would try something that had worked before. She got up, 'Better go now, darling, it's getting late. Think I'll get myself a coffee and turn in..' she faked a yawn. He caught on immediately.

'You can have a coffee with me,' he said, 'At my flat...'

'Is it far?'

'No,' he said.

'Why not? After all, it is Féria, time to let your hair down..' she tossed her glossy hair back from her face. As the full moon illuminated her features he jumped a bit but didn't back off.

One hour later and Trish lay in the big bed covered only by a sheet, her clothes in a heap on the floor. She wore only Daddy's

100

bracelet on her wrist, Daddy wouldn't have liked her to take it off. It had been a failure. He couldn't do it. Trish didn't know why, but then men of his age, it happened. She reached for her bag and looked for a cigarette. Heinrick was in the bathroom, she could hear the toilet flushing. The bedroom door opened and he was silhouetted by the bright light behind him. She saw him now as a lumpen shape, rolls of fat hanging over the towel he had wrapped around himself. He had already made his apologies, did he want to try again?

'Roobiboos?' he asked. She hesitated.

'I don't do anything kinky, darling.'

'No...roobiboos...it's a tea, a bush tea, very calming, would you like a cup?'

'Whatever!' When he went to make the tea she grabbed her clothes and pulled them on, picked up her bag, checked the bracelet was still there and slipped down the staircase and into the night. It was only 4.30, plenty of time to find another lover. She decided she would have another Cuba Libre. After all, Cuba took a lot of liberating.

101

Chapter Ten

What not to wear in August

Pat got up earlier than ever in Summer. It was the parrots that usually did it. There was a very tall date palm growing in the yard (optimistically referred to as a garden) and the head of it was right outside her bedroom on the fourth floor. This profusion of palm leaves and immature dates was alive with green parakeets, and they squawked and chattered and screamed something terrible as soon as dawn started to break. She would get up and make tea and then sit on the terrace, her thin cotton wrap loosely tied around her, watching the birds, which she had to admit, although annoying, were absolutely beautiful. She turned occasionally to look between the two apartment blocks opposite where the slit of a sea view, like a vertical moving postcard, was her only glimpse of the horizon.

Today, like most of the days in the summer, there was no horizon. In fact it looked as though a fishing boat was floating in the white sky. The sea was not bothering to stir itself, it lay grey and still under a thick heavy mist which she knew heralded another unbearably sweaty day. It had been a four litre night. That is, the amount of water in the plastic bottle from the air-con unit amounted to about four litres. Thank God for air-con. Life had been intolerable without it. They had tried everything to get some sleep, fans, damp sheets, having a cold shower before bed. One year they had slept upside down with their feet near the headboard so that the ceiling fan was right over their faces.

Nothing had worked, so Bob had said, 'It's no good, girl, we'll have to raid the bank account and have air-con put in.' What a boon! She was so glad they had done that, the best decision ever.

Talking of decisions she had still not made a move towards grabbing Keith with both hands like Joan had advised. She had been over to the CC twice since, and Joan was always there. The first time she had made a bee line for her table, but she didn't think that Joan remembered her from the first time, she had repeated the same story, almost word perfect, all over again. The next time she avoided her, slipping into Zara's and coming out the other door. She still saw Keith on market days, but it wasn't enough. She just hadn't the courage to make the first move, to ask him back to her flat for tea, or ask him to meet her one evening. She dreamed about it, worked out the words in her head, but worrying about it was now spoiling the relationship, if you could call it that, she wasn't as relaxed in his company as she had been before. All the time she could hear Joan saying "grab him with both hands" over and over again.

* * * * *

Although Malcolm had gone to the UK, Jenny had not. Everybody thought this was strange, but then Jenny was strange, always sitting in the corner, reading, never saying a word. Lynne would study her sometimes, she had a pale complexion, and fine gingery hair. Obviously she had to keep out of the sun, but the books, they always looked new. She put it to Sandra, who was sitting on the terrace while her husband, inside the bar, waffled on to Brian about something or other.

103

'Jenny didn't go back, then?' she enquired, to find out if Sandra knew anything.

'No. Funny, isn't it?' She obviously didn't.

'Those books, she reads loads of them.'

'Well, a lot of people read lots of books, well, they say they read them. I think they just scan them, they can't possibly take it all in. My sister gets through three a week, but she couldn't tell you the plot of any of them. Sometimes she's half way through one before she realises she has read it before.'

'But her books, they are all new, had you noticed? Brand new, hardbacks some of them, and a different one nearly every day...'

Mick was into one of his "not our culture" rants.

'The fiesta is not our culture is it? You can watch it and enjoy the colour and the spectacle but it's not part of your soul is it?' Brian said he thought he knew what he meant, 'However hard you try you will always be an outsider. It's the difference between playing cricket and watching it.'

'That's rubbish, it's just a party!' said Sandra, 'No more than that.'

At that point Andrea and Phil came hurrying along the Paseo. Andrea looked physically excited, she was waving frantically, couldn't get there quick enough.

'I've won a prize!' she declared, out of breath, 'I can't believe it, I've won a prize..'

Phillip didn't look very pleased. He slumped in a chair, looking furious.

'She told me it was going to be a flat screen tele, guess what it

104

is? A bloody make-over.'

Andrea was so thrilled, 'I bought the ticket weeks ago, didn't I, Phil?'

'Weeks ago.' he confirmed.

'Apparently the first name out of the hat hasn't been along to collect their prize so they drew it again! Me! Me!'

She showed Lynne and Sandra the voucher, it was for 100 euros at a place called "Cuti Curls – Nail and Hair Salon".

'I go there,' said Sandra, flashing her elegant hands. Lynne was jealous. Andrea! What a waste. Phil thought it a waste, too.

'Why couldn't they just give us the money? Hundred euros on a hair do..'

'Will you let them cut your pigtail?' asked Sandra, ignoring Phillip.

'I've decided I will. I've been trying to find the courage for a couple of years, now.'

'I think you should go for a whole new look,' said Lynne, 'Don't hold back.'

'And the other thing is...' she gasped, still as giddy as a child, 'Denise and Terry are back over here!' Andrea was always talking about people nobody else knew.

'When?' asked Sandra.   Andrea looked at her big faced watch, 'About now.'

'Andrea,' asked Lynne, 'How do you know these things? Are you psychic?'

'No, she texted me from the airport.'

'Who are Denise and Terry?' asked Brian.

'Oh Denise is very active. On a lot of committees in the UK.

Can't come away very often because she is so busy. She is the chairperson of SAWAG. The Swatcham Anti Windmill Action Group, and lots of other things.'

'And Terry?'

'Well, Terry is...how can I put it.. he's...'

'A miserable sod,' said Phil.

'That's not nice, Phillip. Shall we say he hasn't a lot of personality. He's very quiet.'

'... and miserable. A miserable sod.'

Brian was putting up the umbrellas to shade the tables, Lynne went in to fetch the coffees, nobody wanted bacon sandwiches that day, it was too hot. It was 10.30 and already about 37 degrees.

'God, it was hot yesterday,' said Sandra, 'I went to the loo and I thought for a minute that I had forgotten to put any knickers on. They were so wet with sweat that they were stuck to me like a second skin, I had to peel them off.'

'Too much information,' said Brian, grimacing.

'It's my feet that suffer most,' said Mick, 'They swell up, and my ankles, can't get any kind of shoes on. Shoes that are comfy normally absolutely cripple me..'

'And when you get in the car..' said Phil, 'If you've left it parked in the sun, must be about 130 degrees in there.'

They were discussing how to deal with the unbearable humidity, describing in detail which parts of the body were worse affected by rashes and swellings and assorted afflictions when a couple came into view on the Paseo and Andrea cried,

106

'Yoo-hoo!' It was Denise and Terry. Denise was wearing a grey dress with a grey cardigan buttoned over it. She was tiny and her husband, Terry, was slouching along behind, puffing and blowing and wearing a thin nylon anorak. Lynne could not believe her eyes.

Lynne, always critical of people's appearance, had never seen anything quite like this couple. They came onto the terrace and were shaking hands with the people they knew. Why, in God's name, would anybody want to wear a cardigan in this heat?

Denise was about five feet tall but looked smaller. She was thin to an anorexic standard, and had a beaky face with small black eyes and downy fly away hair. That morning Lynne had seen a baby bird dead on the pavement and the image flashed back into her mind. 'That is what she is like!' she thought, cruelly, 'She is a bony, beaky, baby bird, featherless and grey. Quite an extraordinary looking woman.' Her husband Terry, on the other hand, was a stooped individual who walked in a peculiar way, with his gigantic feet at ten to two. They sat down and he sat almost lifeless, saying nothing while she squawked and preached like a vicar's parrot. She introduced herself to Lynne and Brian, and for a moment she took Lynne's hand. Her hand was icy cold, Lynne shuddered.

'You are freezing!!'

'Oh, I'm always cold. I'm a cold mortal.'

'She's a cold mortal...' repeated Terry.

Lynne went inside for a moment to gather her wits, Brian followed, she turned to him,

'I thought we had some funny looking people for customers but these two take the biscuit. And that voice! It's like nails on glass, sets

107

my teeth on edge!' She had forgotten that Jenny sat in the dark corner. She cupped her hand to her mouth and looked across at her. The book didn't move, but as she turned a page there was the hint of amusement on her pale thin lips. Lynne made no attempt to apologise, even though Brian glowered at her.

* * * * *

Andrea examined her reflection in the mirror on the wardrobe door. She turned her head to and fro, swinging the new auburn bob. It looked good, no doubt about it, though it seemed very odd not to feel the weight of her long plait hitting the back of her shoulders. She felt like a dog that had had his tail docked. Her make-up too was so different. A bit heavy, she thought, but then that wouldn't last, it would be all scrubbed off by tomorrow. No, it was the hair that was the best part of the makeover. Without her glasses she looked even better, but she had to put them on, or everything was fuzzy.

'Phillip..I think I should get some new glasses. I've had these for ages, and they don't go with my new look.'

'Should've gone to Specsavers..' he commented, mimicking a popular TV advert.

'How can I? They are in the UK aren't they?' He had taken no interest in her transformation and though she never expected compliments from him, she thought he could have said more than, 'Bit of a change.' when she'd asked him what he thought.

She started examining the contents of her side of the wardrobe, looking for something decent to wear. She had decided, long since, that

108

shorts on the older woman were not a good idea. Thin legs looked bad in them and fat thighs were worse as the inside of the shorts would somehow work its way between the rolling flesh and get wedged in the crack of the bottom. She had seen so many women wobbling along the Paseo like that, giving the hem of their shorts a surreptitious tug every few minutes. The three quarter trousers, or *piratas,* as the Spanish called them were a better look but she herself favoured the long, full gypsy type skirt. She thought them far more flattering if your legs were a bit like tree trunks, which hers were. In her wardrobe she had about ten of these skirts, in various ethnic prints, which she had tracked down in the Hospice Shop or dug out of the three euro pile of assorted clothes on the market. Of course she still had all her shorts, they were on top of the wardrobe in a suitcase, they never threw anything out.

'Phillip...' she called out, as he was sitting on the balcony, 'You know it's my birthday next month, do you think I could have my present early? I would really like to buy myself something new, a dress perhaps. I don't possess a dress...' There was an extended silence. Then Phil came into the bedroom, he looked angry.

'It's turned your head this makeover thing.'

'I'm not talking lots of money. Pat got a nice dress from the Hospice Shop she...' The argument faded away. It was futile. She turned back to the wardrobe. Phil's collection of shirts hung neatly on the other half of the rail. He had six short sleeved shirts and six long (which he never wore unless he rolled the sleeves up) in faded shades of grey, blue, cream and muted stripes. They were the shirts he used to wear to work at Amalgamated Construction. His office shirts. They were all fraying at the collar and the cuffs of the long sleeved versions had

109

that wrinkling that you get when the interfacing becomes detached from the outer fabric. No amount of ironing could smooth it out. He also had a rack of wide, dull, striped ties that never saw daylight, and three pairs of baggy shorts with multiple pockets. So many pockets that the pockets had little pockets of their own.

'I think you should get yourself some T shirts.' She suggested.

'Why?'

'These shirts. They are not very 'Costa del Sol' are they?' She drew the quotes in the air with her index fingers.

'I don't care. They are comfortable and I'll get T shirts when these wear out.'

Phillip had no interest in clothes at all, he hated the subject. And he had even less interest in spending money on them. Andrea chose the latest of her gypsy skirts, a white top to wear with it, and got changed in silence.

* * * * *

Denise and Terry had an apartment that they only used a couple of times a year, if that. It had been an investment. It was only a few yards from El Marinero. Their children, Kaylie their daughter, and Stuart their son, would use it for holidays with the grandchildren, now numbering six. It was on the second floor of a low rise complex and the access to it was via one flight of steps. All the staircases came down into a central patio area. After unpacking and sorting themselves out they decided to get a late breakfast and came out of their front door with Denise in the lead. For some reason she just stood there. Terry

110

pushed at her back,

'Come on, move..'

'I can't!' she cried, 'I'm stuck.'

'What do you mean, stuck?'

'My feet are stuck to the top step..' She wriggled her toes out of her shoes and jumped back onto the doormat. Terry stood just inside the flat. She bent down. 'There's some sort of superglue or something on the top step.'

'Don't be ridiculous.'

'OK. You try to shift my shoes then.' He pulled and pulled at her shoes until the sole came off. It was then that he saw the maintenance man crossing the patio.

'Hey! Alfonso! *Que pasa?*' he asked and the man turned and then cried out.

'*Ay-eee! Señor, no pase nada en la escalera.. Tu no tiene la carta de la communidad?*' Not understanding Spanish they didn't know what he was talking about, but they did grasp the word *'communidad'.* Alfonso told them in pidgin English to wait ten minutes and held up a tin of something that looked like Unibond adhesive. They went inside.

'Who's the President this year?' Denise squawked, 'This is not good enough, we should have been informed.' Terry picked up the mail they had collected on the way in and hadn't yet opened. One letter informed them, in a kind of strangulated English, that "repears to the ladders are necessario and they are to have adhesivo spread before this can be made good. No use the ladders until after 12 noon" and the date given for the work was that very day.

'Ladders?' asked Denise, 'What are they talking about?'

111

'They must mean stairs. You wait till I see the President, who is,' he scrutinised the signature, 'Herr Klinsman, they should have put a notice up!'

'They'll pay for my shoes, you watch. I'll have the money off them.'

'Too right,' said Terry. When something annoyed him, or something interested him, he became animated and articulate as though someone had thrown a switch. When all was resolved, or a conversation held no relevance to him or his lifestyle he clammed up, went silent and morose as though his battery had run down. Now he was fired up and was waving his arms about and threatening the *Communidad* with all kinds of *denuncias* and letters of complaint. Denise was used to this, in fact she didn't even notice whether he was switched on or off. She changed the tune, having thought about it for a minute.

'Don't make such a fuss. I suppose I've had those shoes since about 1992, I've had my wear out of them. I've got too much to worry about with the wind turbine farm and the gypsies invading the village green, I can't concern myself with a bit of glue and a silly mishap.'

Terry went and sat on the terrace and didn't speak for the rest of the afternoon.

Chapter Eleven

End of Season

August was almost over and now there were a trickle of British tourists coming into El Marinero. Not that there had not been families in the peak of the Summer, poor souls who had no option but to brave the heat as their jobs, or children's schools, required them to take their leave during the high season. It was expensive then, and of course the heat was at its worst, but there were always a few people who actually enjoyed that. Now, as September approached, the more mature holidaymakers were trying out the resort, or returning like birds on a migratory path, to the scene of previous holidays.

The fact that the word September was one that most of the expats longed to see on the calendar did not mean that the hot weather suddenly abated. The energy sapping properties of that big white sun would continue for many weeks yet, but as the nights lengthened at least there was time for things to cool off before dawn broke again. Soon it would be possible to walk on the sand without burning the soles of your feet off, possible to walk a few yards without feeling the need for clean underwear. The permanent lake of sweat in the small of the back and nape of the neck would evaporate and the brain would be able to function on a higher level rather than simply ticking over, full of thoughts revolving around cool drinks, showers and food that somebody else would prepare.

Andrea came into El Marinero with a fresh piece of gossip. Was she connected to some invisible radar? How did she pick these things up?

'Have you heard about Big Mac?' she asked Denise, who was the first person she saw.

'Big Mac? Who's Big Mac?'

'Little Scottish fella — you know — he comes to quiz with his wife and daughters...'

Denise shook her head. Andrea turned on Brian. 'Big Mac.... have you heard?'

'What?' asked Brian. Andrea took a deep breath and began the tale,

'He was on his way to the airport, along the motorway, going to pick up some friends, or it might have been a relation, I'm not sure...'

'And?'

'Car broke down, had to pull onto the hard shoulder.'

'Oh no,' said Denise, trying to be interested, though she didn't know the man to speak to at all, she had seen him but that was it.

'Then a Spanish driver, going like the clappers, runs into the back of Mac's car. Mac gets out and they argue and then Mac smacks him on the nose and they start fighting. The Guardia roll up and arrest both of them, Jean, that is Mrs Mac, just sits there crying her eyes out...'

'So did they get to the airport?'

'No. Course not. The friends had to take a taxi, cost them ninety-five euros.'

114

A couple came onto the terrace and sat under an umbrella. There was no breeze that day and the humidity was high. Andrea and Phil decided to stay inside the bar with the air-con on, though the constant opening and shutting of the door didn't help its efficiency. Lynne went out to serve the couple. At that moment Mick and Sandra trudged into view and got seated, as well as another foursome, who sat themselves around an adjoining table. These four fat pensioners had been customers for the best part of two weeks, and they weren't enjoying their holiday. One of them showed Lynne his legs, livid with big red spots.

'We've been bit to death...' he said, 'Look, all over me they are, itch like bloody hell..' Lynne had to agree it looked nasty, 'My wife's got one on her thigh like an egg, she can't decide whether to pop it or not. I said you'll be home soon, Margaret, take it t'doctor, let him decide.'

'Can't sleep,' she said, 'Itching and sweating. It rubs on the sheets.'

'This is our eighth year, and our last, not coming again I can tell thee.' Lynne took their order for four breakfasts, then turned to Mick, 'Same as usual, Mick?' he nodded. The other couple only wanted coffee at first, then the husband said he fancied a crumpet and she said she would have a toasted teacake.

'Why not!' said the wife, 'He hasn't had a bit of crumpet for years and you've got to have a little of what you fancy on holiday. Let your hair down.'

'Too true,' said Lynne, thinking that if a toasted teacake was letting her hair down she must have led a sheltered life.

The couple turned to Mick.

'We're on the campsite,' said the husband, 'Do you live here?'

Mick puffed himself up ready to offer advice to the uninitiated, his favourite hobby.

'We certainly do.'

'What's it like on the campsite?' asked Sandra, cutting off Mick's lecture before it began.

'Oh, it's alright. We've got our camper van, you see,' the woman nudged her husband in the ribs,

'Tell them,' she said, 'About last night. You know, those people.'

'Oh yes, that was funny that was...this couple rolled up in a really old, clapped out van, you should've seen it. Turns out they bought it on ebay, and after they set off they had only gone five miles and one of the wheels came off...they are on their way to **Bulgaria** in it, with three big rescue dogs. You couldn't swing a cat in it, let alone a big shaggy rescue dog.' Everybody laughed.

'Bulgaria!' said Sandra.

'Yes! I wouldn't have gone as far as Milton Keynes myself.'

'Tell me,' said the wife, 'We are thinking about buying a place here, what sort of thing would you recommend?' This was one of Mick's regular themes.

'Don't buy anything next to a piece of open land. Somebody will build on it. They might tell you it's not possible, but believe me, it is. Don't buy off-plan, that can be a disaster, sometimes the block doesn't get finished, the builder goes broke and you'll not get your deposit

116

back. Also, you might find yourself liable for huge water bills, you can get fined for not paying bills that they haven't even sent you. You could still be on builder's electricity as well. No, don't buy new. Don't buy anything too near the sea, that is illegal and they could demolish it. Buy an older property, but not too old. And not in the *campo*. If you are up the *campo* you have to think about services, say you need to go to the hospital for treatment, the roads can wash away in the Winter, you have to think of all that...'

'Oh, right...' They thought he had finished, but he had only just got started.

'Don't be seduced by a view. A view is fine but only if you are not too isolated. You are better down here, on the coast. And if you fancy a swimming pool, be warned, they can really run away with your money. Even if they are shared pools, part of the *communidad*, when they get old they need relining and it costs a mint. Remember that the Spanish are very loud, very noisy, they will squash twenty people into a two bed place in the summer holidays. Choose somewhere that's mostly English or German. The Germans always make sure everything is maintained, they won't stand for any shoddy workmanship. And don't trust the Notary, it is the man's job to check all the paperwork but if there is something illegal he will probably turn a blind eye and you won't have a leg to stand on if it comes to court. The Notary counts for nothing, but you still have to pay him. You might be asked to pay part of the cost in "black money" that means it doesn't go on the deeds, you hand it over in cash. This is normal practice but illegal. Don't do it if you can avoid it.'

'So all in all...' said the woman, shaken 'You wouldn't

117

recommend it.'

'Oh, no, I didn't say that. You'll love it, it's great. Only be *careful...*' Sandra leaned over and whispered in his ear,

'You bugger! You stamped on their dream.'

Lynne served the pensioners with their breakfasts.

'That's mine,' said the one with the teeth like crooked gravestones, 'No beans and only one sausage.'

'I'm the scrambled egg and two fried slice..' said his wife, hitching up her shorts which were stretched across a balloon-like belly. The woman in the purple sarong pointed to the other plate.

'I'm the bacon very crispy, no tomatoes, mushrooms and plenty of beans...'

'And I'm the as per. As per the menu.' said her husband.

The one with the teeth raised a fork full of yellow yolk to his lips, his hand was quivering slightly, and the yolk dribbled.

'I still think I should pop this thing..' said the woman with the nasty bite.

'Well, if you do, cover it with Savlon or something first, and have a dressing ready,' her friend advised.

'Do you think it will have a lot of little spiders inside?' The fork with the egg stopped in mid journey.

'Shut up, will you, I'm eating. No, it will probably be like that thing from Alien. Go for your throat.' They all tucked into their food, stopping only to remark.

'Bloody hot, 'nt it? I'm not coming next year.'

'No, definitely not.'

118

* * * * *

The Mediterranean diet, olive oil, fresh fruit and vegetables, lots of oily fish and a little lean meat plus lots of carbohydrates all washed down with a little red wine has been declared the healthiest way to eat. This may well have been true in the past when adversity forced the peasants to eat only what they had, and what they had, in that region was a few shellfish, a handful of rice and the products of the *matanza,* the slaughtering of the fatted pig, of which everything was used except the squeak. These days the Mediterranean diet consists of lots of white bread, olive oil, dozens of eggs, some salad, kilos of commercially produced phosphate and salt loaded *embutidos,* (that is, a hundred different kinds of luncheon meat, *chorizo* and sausages) and lots of fish and seafood deep fried in batter and served with chips. All vegetables were stewed until they disappeared altogether. Not to mention the international lure of the hamburger, pizza and chicken chow mein which had invaded the traditional fare, along with chocolate loaded bread, biscuits and lots of very sweet cakes with artificial cream. Obesity in Spain was now on the rise.

When Denise and Terry went out for a meal it was always a complicated matter. To start with she was a vegetarian, not quite a vegan but not far off for she ate very little dairy produce. Terry on the other hand was what you would call a "picky eater". He had hygiene issues, and problems with food not being fresh or prepared correctly. He wouldn't eat frozen food, he wouldn't eat anything microwaved. Mrs

119

Jenkins, their neighbour had used her microwave every day and now she was dead from cancer. He couldn't stand garlic. He hated sauces. Meat had to be cooked until no blood was showing. Fish had to have bones and head removed. If there were peanuts on the table he had to have a spoon in the dish, because he didn't do finger food or sharing. The way these Spanish all dipped into the piles of battered fish bits, the salad and the bread, everything shared from plates in the centre of the table, handled by everyone; he thought it disgusting.

Fed up with listening to Andrea going on about her makeover, and different people coming into El Marinero with new versions of the Big Mac story, Denise and Terry decided they would chance their arm at going out for something to eat, so they went next door for lunch.

Terry studied the menu in La Abuela's, the favourite Spanish restaurant of the ex-pat crowd.

'What's "arm of lamb"?' he asked. Denise thought for a minute.

'I suppose they mean shoulder.' There was a pause while they read on.

'It says "Goldfish"! They can't mean goldfish, surely, not like you get in an aquarium...and what's this? "Blacksmith"? For God's sake what's Blacksmith?'

'Where?' he showed her the entry, 'Some kind of fish, I suppose, it's in the Fish Section..' He carried on looking, the waiter came over and he shooed him away.

' How about "Pig on Iron garrisoned by Salad"? Does that sound appetising?'

'I don't know why you are looking at those dishes, how do you know they are fresh? How do you know they won't contain garlic or be smothered in sauce?'

'I don't even know what they are, let alone whether they are fresh. "Shrimps in overcoats" ?' Denise sighed.

'There's nothing here for me. If I order a salad how do I know they won't put tuna on it? They think tuna is a vegetable, you always get it on a salad.'

'Watch it! If you order salad it will be a big one to share. I'm not sharing.'

'I could have the aubergines with honey...'

'Do you like that?'

'I don't know. Might do...'

'Stick to *garbanzos..*'

'Chick peas...don't they cook them in stock with *chorizo?*'

'I'll have a *racion* of ham and a *racion* of cheese...'

'And I'll have a *tortilla*. They can't mess up an omelette, can they?'

'So will I, I'll have a *tortilla.*'

Which was the decision that they always came to, every time they went out for a meal.

* * * * *

Incidentally, Brian was so sick of the Big Mac story that he had decided to keep count of the number of people who related it by making a mark with a biro on a beer mat. By teatime he had recorded

121

six versions and it was morphing, too, Mac had punched the Guardia, Mrs Mac had been injured, and the Spanish driver was drunk. By the end of the week, he thought, Mac would be dead, the driver would be unmasked as Fernando Alonso and Mrs Mac, desperate for income, would have opened a haggis stand on the Paseo.

Chapter Twelve

All Together Now

It was such a lovely warm evening that Pat decided to go for a stroll along the Paseo. This was the last weekend before all the Spanish tourists went back to their homes in order to get their children ready for the new term. Three solid months they had been off school, just imagine it, and not a minute's break from their attentions as no Spanish parents ever put their kids to bed before they turned in, meaning that the mothers had them to deal with during their every waking hour, often up until two or three in the the morning. What a life, she thought, no peace at all. What a commitment. She found herself a place under a mimosa tree, her favourite spot. The leaves were dense and the shade they offered more so. She could sit there, on "her" wall, the piercing rays of the setting sun unable to touch her. It was still hot, and Spanish families were trudging down to the beach with their sunshades, aluminium folding chairs, insulated boxes, granny, the inflatable killer whale, three children and the baby with all his necessary paraphernalia. It used to seem strange that they went to the beach when there was only about an hour's daylight left, when all British people had come off the sand and gone to their hotels to get washed. Sensible, really, but then the sun always seemed hotter when it was full in your face, hotter than midday, Pat thought.

She was looking across the beach at the colourful display of sunshades and sun beds. These days they all looked newly bought, they had trendy fluorescent colours, subtle pastels, stripes and checks and clean white fringes. Only a few years ago they would have been faded, second season versions of promotional material, every one of them carrying an advertisement for Coca Cola, or brands of beer, ice tea or water. Begged, stolen or borrowed from some bar or restaurant then, now people had the money to buy brand new, and the big rubbish containers would be brimming with broken chairs, discarded brollies and punctured lilos after the exodus back to Córdoba and Sevilla.

Near the water's edge a party of children in red T shirts sat in a circle. They were probably on an exchange visit, children from Orilla went inland and they came here for their first view of the sea. The Church organised it. She then saw something that made her double take. A nun, in a starched white habit, was walking across the beach towards these children carrying a six foot long rubber crocodile under her arm. Pat laughed out loud, how Bob would have liked to see that, a nun and a crocodile. A hand on her shoulder made her start and she turned to see...Keith!

Was he an hallucination? Were the nun and the crocodile and Keith all part of some bizarre dream? Then he spoke.

'Sorry to make you jump,' She swivelled round on the wall until her feet were back on the Paseo.

'That's OK, I was just looking at...' she pointed in the direction of the nun, but she had disappeared into thin air...'There was a nun with a.....' she didn't say crocodile, he might think she was mad, 'How are you?'

'Oh, not too bad. The old ticker has been playing up a bit, went to the doc and she gave me new pills. Fit as a flea, now. I...er...I was going for a spot of dinner. I would love you to join me.' Had all her Christmases come at once? To meet up, so unexpectedly and then to be asked to go for a meal. She had already eaten but she didn't tell him that.

'I'd love to, although I haven't come dressed for a restaurant, and I haven't brought any money I...'

'You look lovely as always. And it's my treat. Do you like Chinese?' She said she did and they walked together along the Paseo until they reached the New Yang Chinese Restaurant. Was it really happening? At last they were together without pretending to be casual people who just met on market days. She had been invited, and he was paying, it could definitely be considered a date.

They sat outside on the terrace, he with his back to the Paseo, and Pat facing him at a table for four. Bigger tables are better, he said, as they can never fit all the food on one hotplate, you need space for two. Conversation flowed easily, she told him of her week, of the Big Mac story, of Denise and Terry and the steps, all the gossip that had filtered its way through the many layers of people who were connected by nothing more than rumours and anecdotes about each other. It was then that she saw them, slowly gliding along, hand in hand, it was Andrea and Phil coming their way. Oh no! She thought, if they see us together it will be all over Orilla before I get home. She excused herself and rushed into the toilet at the back of the restaurant weaving between an army of empty tall-backed chairs crammed together as if they were expecting ten coach parties all at once. She waited in the ladies room, checking her lipstick and combing her hair slowly, with one eye on her

125

watch. Surely they would have gone by now. She peered out of the toilet but couldn't see past the serried ranks of stiff chairs, so she counted to ten and walked back to the terrace. There they were, Andrea and Phil talking to Keith. How did they know him? He said he didn't use the Marinero much, they never used Emilio's? She had to walk over to her seat then.

'Hello, Pat,' said Andrea, the low sun making her made-over hair, by now a bit unkempt, look even redder, 'Out for a nice Chinese?'

'Yes, how are you?'

'We're fine. On our way to see Mick and Sandra, we're all going to La Abuela's, it's Mick's birthday..'

'Oh, really. Do you know Keith?'

'Yes, long time no see, though, isn't it Keith?' and with a wink they continued on their way. Why, oh why did they have to spoil her evening? Now she would be worrying all night about the rumours going around. Keith gave her a menu,

'Do you like Peking duck?' he asked, and she answered,

'Very much indeed. It was Bob....' she was going to say "Bob's favourite", but, no, leave Bob out of it tonight, she thought, tonight is just for me and Keith.

* * * * *

Roger liked to keep an eye out for Pat. He admired how she had coped after Bob's sudden demise, and how she never said a bad word about anybody. He tried to help where he could although she never turned to him for assistance. It was quiz night and he rang her to check if she wanted a lift. Normally, this time of year, she would say that she was happy to walk but she jumped at the suggestion, telling him she had something to tell them. Julie, too, had something up her sleeve. They picked her up at the corner of her street.

'I met a friend the other night..' she said, 'By accident. We speak sometimes when our paths cross, anyway he...'

'Oh, it's a "he"...' said Julie, knowingly.

'Well, that's the point. He asked me to go for a Chinese and guess who should see us? Andrea and Phil. I just wanted to say that if you hear rumours about me having a "boyfriend", there's nothing in it... it's just...'

' "Boyfriend" I always think they should invent a better name, when older people are involved..' said Julie, 'Don't worry, Pat, we know you are not doing anything untoward. Actually, I wanted to ask you a favour. I'm going to start doing Spanish lessons and I'm looking for somewhere to hold them. We can't do them at home,'

'People would have to get up the mountain..' explained Roger.

'And we know you have a big living room.'

'Oh, please! I would love you to do them at my flat! And I'll join, if that's OK...are you going to charge?'

'I don't think so, not yet anyway. All we'd need is a cup of tea and a biscuit, I can give you some money for that.'

'No, don't be silly, I can run to cups of tea. In fact I could bake a cake, I'm a good cake maker, and it would give me a chance to keep my hand in.'

'We don't want to put you to any trouble.'

'I shall really enjoy it,' she said, 'Thank you for thinking of me.'

* * * * *

It was Dan's first go at compiling the quiz and he had spent lots of time on it. He had got questions off the Internet, cut photos from magazines and pasted them up, and run off answer sheets on his printer. He had been warned that at the September quiz when everybody was back together there would be more teams than usual, as people would come along just to be reunited with those returning from the rain and the assorted rigours of the United Kingdom. He was prepared for twelve teams, and really looking forward to it.

When Roger, Julie and Pat arrived they were amazed by the number of people. All the usual faces plus some holidaymakers, all the tables were taken inside and out. They had to do some table shifting, and moving of chairs in order to find a little space. Andrea, heading towards the toilet at the back, waved at Pat as she went by. Pat was glad she wasn't nearer, so she could comment. Malc was talking to Mick.

'Spain won, then, after all. Dirty game, though. I knew the Dutch would crock them.'

'Terrible. Should have been down to nine men. I think he did well, though, Harold the ref. He should have sent him off for that karate kick but he gave them a second chance.'

'Good job the Dutch didn't win. Can you imagine the inquest?'

'Great night though, they were papping their horns, driving round, singing and cheering into the early hours. *Campeones del Mundo.*'

'Not a good tournament though, all in all.'

'Nobody played well.' Mick had to agree, 'And Spain were really Barcelona with a few extras. That was the difference, they were used to playing as a team.'

Dan started the quiz. The silence after each question seemed to indicate that people were struggling. They certainly couldn't make head nor tail of the photo round, and now Dan's Geography Round had them completely stumped. He also had to read all the questions twice, as there were teams both inside and outside. They were half way through when a noise was heard, a banging.

'What's that noise?' asked Lynne, sticking her head out of the kitchen door. She was busy trying to do more refreshments, not having expected so many people to turn up.

'Help!' came Andrea's strangulated voice, 'I'm stuck in the lavatory!' Everybody laughed and Brian had to go and put his shoulder to it. Andrea emerged, red faced,

'Phillip! Why didn't you come and rescue me?' Phillip shrugged.

'He thought you were having another make over..' said a voice from somewhere.

'Sorry,' said Lynne, 'I've told Brian to fix that door, but he won't do it.'

'I haven't had time to do it.' Brian added, annoyed.

'Oh, I feel quite faint.. ' Andrea said, 'I think I better have a small brandy.'

'Small brandy on the house, coming up..' said Lynne, casting Brian a black look.

129

While the refreshments were being served Julie put a notice on the board and then stood up and clapped her hands to get attention.

'I just want to say that I know a lot of you struggle with Spanish, so next month I am going to start doing Spanish classes. There is a notice on the board, please leave your name and number and I'll ring you when I've set everything up. Thank you.'

The first person to put their name down was Jenny. It was the first time she had ever been to a quiz night and here she was getting involved. She left her seat, walked to the board, wrote her name and number and sat down again. Jenny, who never said a word in English to anybody, wanted to learn Spanish! This will be interesting, thought Roger, who had been press-ganged into joining the class himself, he'd never even heard her speak.

* * * * *

Things had returned to normal. It was now possible to park, even at weekends. The beaches were almost empty and the weather was nigh on perfect, cloudless skies and only thirty degrees. Just bearable, perfect holiday weather and yet the bulk of the tourists had gone home.

Mick and Malc were holding court again, sitting on the terrace, legs akimbo, bacon sandwiches to sustain them.

'The world is obsessed with communication,' said Mick, 'It's not necessary. Why do people feel that they have to be in touch with everybody they know (and lots of people they don't know, come to that) every minute of every day. We lived for years without a telephone, let

130

alone a mobile.'

'Telephones were a luxury. Even at work. You only used them if it was an absolute necessity.' Malc remembered.

'Quite. And then there's the computer. Why is it essential to be on the computer all the bloody time? Take my brother, Willy, he's on that computer all hours God sends. He's got nothing to tell me but I keep getting emails "Bet it's warmer there than here" that sort of thing.' Sandra interrupted his rant.

'That's 'cause he's stuck in front of the computer. It's his life. He is disabled, in a wheelchair,' she said, disgusted. She liked Willy.

'That's as maybe. But what I am saying is wasn't the world a nicer place when you could ignore people and get a bit of peace?'

'I'd like a bit of peace from you,' said Sandra.

A couple came onto the terrace, the man was carrying a fishing rod. They sat down and Lynne took their order.

'Lovely day..' the woman said to Malc, looking for a conversation, 'Bit hot but...'

'This is cool, love, only about 30 today. This is nothing to what we're used to.'

'How would you know?' said Mick, 'Where were you when it was 39? In the UK, that's where. In Godalming.'

'It's not Godalming, it's Godmanchester.'

'You live here then?' They all confirmed they did. 'What do you miss most about England, then?'

'Common sense,' said Mick, 'There's not much of it about.'

'Parsnips,' said Sandra,

131

'You can get parsnips..' Malc interrupted, 'Jenny got some on the market.'

'Can you? Well, then...er...smoked haddock.'

'You can get that,' said the woman tourist, 'From that English shop, what's it called "Gooseberries" ?.

'That's something you can't get, except in a tin..' said Sandra, 'I love a gooseberry crumble.'

'When you miss a product, though,' said Malcolm who had come back from the UK with a case full of teabags, ginger nuts and butter puffs, 'It gets out of all proportion in your mind, you remember it, not as it is now but as it was when you were a kid,' They nodded, sagely, 'But then you are always disappointed when you get it, and think, what was all the fuss about?'

'That's an old adage,' said Mick, 'That things are different, they haven't altered them at all..'

'Oh, yes they have!' they all cried, 'Look at Wagon Wheels, they used to be HUGE, and Lucozade, that was delicious, now it tastes like...well...any other pop.' said the woman.

'Spam's not the same,' added Sandra, 'Nothing like! And Mars bars; the toffee part used to be half of it, now it's only the top bit.' They all took a minute to think about this. Mick turned to the man with the fishing rod.

'Going fishing?'

'I hope so,' he said, 'Do you know where I can fish, a reservoir or somewhere?'

'Reservoir! No chance. You'll need a licence to fish, even on the beach..'

'Really?'

'Oh, yes. If you want to do fresh water fishing you have to take an *exam.*'

'No!' Mick and Malc nodded in unison, then Malc explained.

'You need a licence for everything here mate. You need a licence to fart in this Country.'

Chapter Thirteen

To Be or To Be

It was some days before Lynne noticed that Jenny wasn't accompanying Malc any more on their breakfast trips. She didn't like to ask why, but after the shock of Jenny's name going down on the list of Spanish students, everybody was curious as to why she had suddenly decided to join something. Then, one afternoon when Lynne was just going back to the flat for a shower and to freshen up, Jenny came in on her own.

'Cup of tea,' please.' she asked. Lynne couldn't bear it any longer, she had to know.

'I see you've put your name down for Julie's classes..'

'Yes, thought it was about time,' she had a gentle, quiet voice, quite refined.

Lynne pushed Brian aside and took over the tea making. 'We haven't seen you in the mornings, have you been ill?'

'Ill? No, I've just retired that's all. Turned 60, on the pension now so I've given up my job.'

'Job?'

'Yes, I was a professional book reviewer for a Publishing House. Got too much, I just couldn't get through the books quickly enough for them. You've seen me reading? That was my work.'

'Oh, we just thought you were a bookworm.'

'Yes, I suppose I should've explained. Anyway, I've given that up.

134

Now I can get to learn a bit about Spain.'

'Is Malcolm pleased? That you have retired?'

'No idea,' then Jenny worked it out, that look on Lynne's face, 'You didn't think Malcolm was my husband?'

'Isn't he?'

'No way..he's my brother. Half brother actually. I bought the two apartments, they're side by side, some years ago as an investment and when his wife, Muriel, died we both came out here to live. Malcolm!! God, I couldn't live with him for five minutes.'

The names on Julie's list were Roger (press-ganged), Pat (providing tea and cakes), Sandra and Jenny. To this were added a couple from the Hospice Shop, a woman called Anne and her husband Tony. This was enough to start with, Julie thought. She took a lot of trouble with her text books devising the first lesson. She had never taught anything before, but had been a student in enough classes to know how it worked. Of course this bunch of people wouldn't make up an average class, Julie had no idea how much, or how little, most of them knew, so she had passed around a form asking them to state what level they were at. Tony was "intermediate" according to his wife, who filled it in for him, though she confessed to knowing "very little". The old statement that "I know a lot of words but can't join them up into sentences," was offered by Sandra and then copied out by Pat as well. But Jenny, in a tiny hand, had written a whole paragraph about having learned at school and even that she had taken evening classes.

It wasn't what Jenny, the mystery woman, had written that fascinated Julie, it was her incredible handwriting. The spidery, pencilled

135

writing was quite beautiful, she thought. The small rolling letters in perfect lines with tall 't's carrying long curving crosses, like medieval flags on masts. It looked like the Spanish Armada was sailing across the page. She stared at it for a long time before reading a single word.

* * * * *

'You're not doing Julie's class, then?' Lynne asked Andrea.

'No, I thought about it, but I think I know enough. What I do is I learn a new word every day.'

'That's interesting. So what's today's word?'

'Today's word is *"todavia".*' Lynne was impressed.

'And what does that mean?'

'It means "still going on",'

'In what sense?'

'Well, like "the meeting was still going on", or "they were still eating their meal",'

'Oh, I get it. So what was yesterday's word, then?'

'Yesterday's word was.....' she paused for quite a long while, then had to admit, 'Oh, I can't remember.' Sandra joined in the conversation,

'My problem is that I can't learn long words all at once, my memory is crap. So what I do is split them in half, for example, I could never remember *meer-colas*. So I have to learn '*meer*' and then '*colas*'.. you see, split it up.'

'So what does *meercolas* mean?' asked Lynne.

'Well, it's Tuesday isn't it? Or is it Wednesday?'.

'I'd like to join the class, said Lynne, but with the bar to run I couldn't spare the time.' She cast a black look at Brian, 'Brian wouldn't let me go.'

'You can go if you want, we could do with somebody who could understand the Ice Man.'

'Oh, nobody can understand him!' cried Andrea, 'Even Phil and he's very good at Spanish.'

'Are you Phil?' asked Brian.

'Well, I know a lot of words but I can't make them into sentences,' he said, predictably, 'It's the verbs that throw me out. Can't get the hang of them at all.'

* * * * *

Pat looked around her living room, it looked fine, she thought. She and Bob had taken a lot of trouble selecting furnishings and it was a spacious apartment. They had chosen it because it was roomy, in the newer blocks you got two bathrooms and three bedrooms all crammed into a smaller space than her living room alone. It was a fairly old block, about twenty years old, and showing signs of wear, but they had completely "reformed" (as the Spanish say) throwing out all the furniture and fittings that the previous occupants had left them. The dining table had pull out leaves and this was the first time she had ever used them. She sat six chairs around the table all facing one way. In the kitchen her fruit cake was cut and sliced, her cups all at the ready. The buzzer on the front entrance door sounded, she let Julie and Roger in.

'Look what we found in a skip,' said Roger, holding up a child's blackboard and easel. It had the alphabet printed on it, numbers and a clock face with movable hands.

'Just till we get a proper one..' said Julie. She looked nervous, Pat thought.

'Six isn't it? Plus teacher?'

'Lynne might come, she said she'd try.'

'Oh, seven, and I haven't got another chair..'

'Don't worry, said Roger, if she comes I'll sit on that pouffe.'

Lynne didn't come of course, but all the others arrived in quick succession. Julie was wondering if she should have restricted it to people she knew, this man Tony, Anne's husband, whom she had never met, arrived with a battered briefcase full of text books and folders, pencils and sharpeners, note books and a huge dictionary. He piled them all up neatly, he even had the book "500 Spanish Verbs" to refer to. She looked at Roger, he knew what she was thinking, had this man come determined to prove he knew more than she did?

'Before we start, I would like to thank Pat for the use of her apartment.' A ripple of applause ran round the group. 'Most of you know each other,' she said, 'Most of you are complete beginners and for those who do know a little please bear with us until we have gone through the basics.'

'It doesn't hurt to keep going over the basics,' said Tony, 'I assume we will start with the alphabet.' Julie was annoyed, did he want to run the class?

'No.'

'Oh, only they always start with the alphabet. I've done all the courses, I've done courses on TV, Lingaphone, even the free classes put on for foreigners by the Town Hall and they always...'

'Oh, I went to one of them,' said Sandra, 'Absolutely useless. Nobody spoke any English so you had to know quite a lot to be able to follow the lesson at all.'

'Bet they started with the alphabet?' Tony asked. Julie decided to put a stop to this before it started, she raised her voice.

'We are NOT starting with the alphabet,' she said firmly. The room fell silent. Then she cleared her throat, 'I am sure that you are aware,' she began, conscious that her voice had risen a half tone and sounded rather patronising, 'That languages develop over time. They are constantly changing. Of course Spanish and English both have the same Latin root which should help us but the words that change the most are those that are most used, so the most common verbs, for example, are the most irregular...' She had lost them already, she started to panic. 'For example, the verb "to be" is quite irregular, in fact in Spanish there are two verbs "to be".' She turned to the little board, her chalk was fresh out of the packet and wouldn't write, it squeaked on the painted surface.

'Try breaking it..' Sandra suggested, Julie cracked the chalk in half, it worked, she wrote, *ESTOY* − I AM and then, underneath it *SOY* − I AM.'

'What, soy, like the sauce?' asked Pat, still thinking about Chinese meals.

'I don't get it,' said Sandra, 'How can they both mean the same?'

'*ESTOY* is used when you are referring to something temporary, like "I am ill", that would be "*estoy enferma*" but if you were a permanent invalid it would be "*soy enferma*".' Did they get that? She

139

thought not.

Tony then added,

'Unless you are a man.' Julie glared at him, she knew what he was getting at but didn't want to complicate things further, 'Then it would be ·*estoy enfermo*' or '*soy enfermo*', i.e. It would end in 'o' and not 'a'.' He rocked back on his chair and took a sip from the bottle of water he had brought with him, pleased with himself.

'Can I ask a question?' asked Roger, trying to get back on track. Julie nodded.

'Does everybody know what is meant by a verb? It has been a long time since we were at school, it is possible that some of us need to go over that.' Julie knew that he was trying to tell her that she was getting nowhere. Pat, very bravely raised her hand,

'I'm not sure of those things.' Then Jenny spoke, clearly and sensibly.

'I am not trying to alter your lesson plan, Julie, but I have been on a couple of courses and I can tell you, from experience, that people in general find the verbs very difficult. Perhaps you could introduce them at a later stage.' Julie knew she was right, what had made her think that they would be able to grasp such difficult concepts on the first lesson? But she didn't want to admit she was wrong in front of Tony.

'You should start with the alphabet,' he said.

'Oh, shut up!' said his wife, Anne, suddenly, 'You've been on all these courses yet you daren't open your mouth in public and speak to anybody. So what good has it done?'

'Is it too early for a cup of tea?' asked Pat.

'No,' said Roger, I think that is a very good idea,' and followed

140

her into the kitchen.

After the tea break Julie just about pulled herself together and they did the part of the lesson that concerned naming objects in the room. That went much better, but she felt humiliated and disheartened. It was obvious that some of them couldn't remember the simplest words, when asked to repeat them they sounded different every time. They also couldn't grasp the concept of 'male' and 'female' nouns. When she had held up a plastic bag, for example, everybody who had ever been shopping knew it was "*bolsa*". Tony had to point out that she should always refer to nouns with their definite article, "*la bolsa*" for example, feminine. She told him that they would discuss this later. When she held up her handbag, they all said "*bolsa*" again, and she had to correct them, saying it was in this case "*bolso*", masculine, "*el bolso*".

'I don't get that,' Sandra said, how can a handbag possibly be masculine?'

'Unless it's a man bag,' said Roger.

* * * * *

Back home she slumped into a chair, looking vacant. Now Julie never slumped, and she never looked vacant.

'Don't be upset,' said Roger, pouring her a glass of white wine, 'It was OK, in the end.'

'They didn't get it, I thought I had it all worked out in easy stages I....'

141

'If you want my opinion,'

'Might as well, I've had everybody else's,' she snapped.

'If you want my opinion you shouldn't have started with the verb "to be", in fact you shouldn't plunge them into verbs straight off, Jenny was right, that is the reason most people drop out of Spanish classes. They didn't have your education, and if they did they can't remember their English grammar.'

'But you HAVE to do verbs..'

'Not all at once, start slowly. Start with an easy one like *HABLAR* to speak, it's regular and you can do it in easy stages, 'I speak, you speak' one week, then 'we speak, they speak' another, get it?'

'That's the only verb you ever mastered..' she laughed, remembering her attempts to teach him some years ago.

'Proves it's easy, then.'

'Trouble is, they probably won't come again.'

'Oh, they'll come. That was the most fantastic fruit cake.' She had to agree, Pat had done them proud.

Chapter Fourteen

Absent-mindedness

When Pat had nightmares now it was not about that terrible day when she had discovered her husband of forty two years dead in their bed. Her nightmares were of endless corridors with long queues, battling through crowds of waiting people to speak to a rude, miserable person whose only claim to being loftier than her was that they were in possession of a rubber stamp. In her dreams she would be hurtling through traffic in Elsie's car, gripping the thick grey folder into which she had packed her passport, expired residencia card and papers, bus pass, bank statements, utility bills and every conceivable document she thought they might ask for including her Co-op Divi card from 1968 and a completely full book of Green Shield Stamps. And always there was something else they wanted, with photocopies and verification from some lawyer or other bureaucrat, and she would have to pay them to sign it.

If they had known that a joint account was not joint, and a joint ownership was a shared ownership she doubted seriously if they would have gone through with the move in the first place. Like many others before them they had thought that two names on a document meant that both people owned it all, and if one of them died the other became the sole owner. They had no idea that it meant that you owned half each and if one person went "to the glory" as the Spanish say, you paid tax on the half that you "inherited". Pat thought this was a

143

barbaric law, and should be reported to the European Court of Human Rights.

She had had one of those dreams last night, and they always left her feeling spaced out and anxious. She couldn't quite wake up from them, because it brought it all back. Why did Spanish people in positions of power have to be so odious? She'd asked Mick that once because he had an answer for everything and he said, facetiously, that they sent them on an Obstructive Behaviour Course. It seemed that way, because normally they were polite and kind, helpful and pleasant. In all the shops and restaurants she had encountered nothing but friendly, helpful people but as soon as they got a job in the public sector they changed and did their utmost to make you suffer. All that queuing, the Spanish would queue for days, literally, and they seemed so patient. But if they were driving behind you they would pap their horns and overtake, even at crossings, they couldn't wait a minute. It's the Franco Syndrome, Bob used to say, they are still afraid that if they complain the authorities will have them shot.

She had sorted out some of Bob's DVD's to give to the Hospice Shop and was going to take them there that morning. Bob liked violent films, war stuff and gangsters but she didn't. He used to watch them while she went to bed with a Catherine Cookson. She put them into a carrier bag and was bagging up her *basura,* her rubbish, when the doorbell rang. It was Mrs Gonzales.

'*Buenas dias..*' said the neighbour and handed Pat a huge carrier bag bursting with tomatoes. Pat thanked her and she left. It was nice of her to give Pat all these fruits but what did you do with them? She had been brought up not to waste food and couldn't bear to throw any

144

of it away so she lined them all up on the work top in the kitchen. There must have been five kilos of them, some misshapen, some green, some red. They were the tomatoes that were left on the vines in the polythene greenhouses, when they cleared them out the workers helped themselves or they would all be thrown away. Whatever would her mother say if she could see so much wastage? She selected a few nice ones to eat, a few more to cook with but there was still about four kilos left. The most annoying part was that she had bought tomatoes only the day before. Then she had an idea, Elsie and Ivy.

Taking her key she locked the flat and went down in the lift to the first floor where Elsie and Ivy had their flat. She rang the bell and Ivy answered it. She liked Ivy, she was softly spoken and not abrasive like her sister.

'Would you like some tomatoes?' Ivy pointed to a lumpy carrier bag in the hall,

'Mrs Gonzales just brought us these.'

'Oh. What can you do with so many tomatoes?' said Pat. Elsie appeared behind her sister.

'Make soup,' she said, it is amazing how many tomatoes you can use up by making soup.'

'But I don't fancy soup in this weather, it's much too hot, and I certainly don't want to stand making it.'

'You could bottle them. That's what we did in the war.' said Elsie.

'But if you bottle them you know you won't have used them up when she comes and gives you another five kilos.'

'It's good of her,' said Ivy, 'It's the five kilos of cucumbers that are the worst.'

145

They all agreed.

'What do you do with yours? Make *gazpacho?*'

'No. We throw most of them away,' said Ivy, honestly, 'After we've kept them for a bit.'

'It's such a shame when food is getting dearer all the time,' Pat reflected.

'If you want to save money then you must "think Spanish" ' said Elsie, 'That's what I do. I don't buy English in the supermarkets. And I wouldn't go to that "Blackberries" shop or whatever it's called, they are too expensive.'

'It's "Gooseberries.." ' said Pat.

'Well, whatever it's called. No, we eat what the natives eat, garlic, chicken, sardines. We don't buy English.'

'Except tea bags,' said Ivy, 'And Oxo...'

'Well, except those. And bacon of course.'

'What about sausages?' Pat enquired as she didn't trust Spanish sausages.

'Sometimes. What I do I drive down to Gibraltar every couple of months and stock up in Morrison's. Just the essentials. You can come with us next time if you like'. Pat declined the offer. Pat was no financial genius but she could handle her housekeeping money and couldn't see that driving to Gibraltar for a box of teabags could save more money than shopping in Gooseberries. Not when you took the petrol into account.

Having collected her bags from the flat she locked up and went out. There were two entrances to her block, the back gate led into a road that passed behind several other blocks and the front gate out to

146

the main road which connected to the Paseo and the centre of the town. She went out the front way. She couldn't shake off the remnants of her dream and also she couldn't stop thinking that although she had given Keith her number he hadn't rung her once. She was hoping he might ask her round to meet Poppy, the dog, or suggest another meal together. She felt it was too forward to ring him, and was growing increasingly uneasy, thinking that perhaps he didn't really like her after all.

The machine that swept the gutters came rumbling along the street, sucking up dust at the front and spilling it out the other end. The "dust distributor" is what Bob had Christened it. This always made her smile, and with her mind brimming with all these thoughts she put her foot on the pedal of the giant communal wheelie bin and threw both her rubbish and the bag with the DVDs inside. She clapped her hand to her mouth and gave a sharp intake of breath. Luckily she still had her shoulder bag which was strung, anti-mugger fashion, across her chest.

Mrs Gonzales put down her hose pipe and it squirmed and danced on the pavements, splashing water at the feet of passersby who swore and jumped back from its deluge. She rushed over as she had seen what Pat had done and produced a mobile phone from the pocket of her baggy *bata,* the loose house dress favoured by Spanish housewives of a certain age. She speed dialled her son Diego and when he answered she shouted into it, asking him to come down. Pat could hear both ends of the conversation because Diego was standing on the first floor balcony above them and shouting just as loud. There was no need for telecommunication.

Diego was a big, slightly retarded young man with long arms and

147

a bulk gained from consuming too many bread rolls with chocolate fillings. He lumbered onto the scene wearing a red "*Campeones del Mundo*" T shirt that was two sizes too small. His mother shouted at him to get his hands into the bin and rescue the things for the lady. The bin was as tall as Pat and, having been emptied during the night (as it was every night of the year bar New Year's Eve) there was little in it. Pat peered inside and the rotten smell of prawn heads and decomposing vegetables made her reel back.

'The *verde..*' she said, pointing to the green carrier bag. Diego hooked it out with the tips of his fingers and she thanked him profusely, taking one of the DVD's and giving it to him, but Mrs G. took it off him and gave him a hefty slap.

'*Muy mal...muy mal..*' she repeated, '*No regalo par el*' and pushed him back towards the flat. Pat, relieved, thanked her as profusely as her Spanish would allow and Mrs Gonzales went back to her hosepipe which had, by now, flooded the entire street.

* * * * *

Roger, on his way to pick up Julie from the Hospice Shop, took a few minutes to sit on a bench by a huge hibiscus bush that was absolutely covered in pale pink trumpets with red throats. He stretched his left leg out to ease the pain in his knee which still bothered him from time to time. He had had an unsuccessful morning trying to fathom something out on the computer and it always irked him when he couldn't cope with modern technology. After all, at work, years ago, he had been one of the first people to learn the computers. They were huge things with green screens in those days and when you wanted them to do something you had to write an encoded command before they would perform. He got very good at this and was considered the "Centre of Excellence" in the company, with other departments all turning to him for computer help. Then he had had the bad car accident which smashed up his leg and resulted in him being off work for eighteen months, and only just being able to walk when he went back. In that short time computers had evolved in leaps and bounds and after having once been the font of all IT knowledge he found himself barely able to operate one at all. He'd felt emasculated by this and had got very depressed, his new boss shipping him here and there and giving him all the work nobody else wanted to take on. Julie had been marvellous in those months when he was at home, the boys, Michael and Jonathon, were teenagers then and quite a handful. Julie had been his rock.

Roger checked his watch, and remembered that a vital piece of household equipment, the corkscrew, had broken the night before and he had promised to buy a new one. All over Orilla there were "Chinese" shops selling everything under the sun. Many of these were run by Moroccans rather than actual Chinese people but the goods all came from China. He went into one such "Bazaar" passing as he did so a machine for blowing up lilos and other rubber seaside novelties. The aisles seemed to get narrower every time he went into this shop and the range of goods more varied. He was searching for a corkscrew amongst the kitchen gadgets at the end of the first aisle when a woman with a child in tow came up to him and asked,

'*Compresas?*' Why did they always ask him things, when he

was walking along the street they would pull over in their cars and ask him the way. Why? Did he look Spanish with his fair hair and blue eyes? He couldn't have looked more British had he been wearing a Union Flag T shirt and a kilt. He assumed the woman wanted to know where she could inflate her daughter's dolphin or some such so he took her and pointed to the large compressor near the doorway. She frowned. Luckily the shop keeper came over and when the woman asked again for *compresas,* she glowered at Roger and took the customer down another aisle. Curious, he peeped round the corner and saw the assistant hand her a packet of sanitary towels. He left quickly, without his corkscrew, and laughed all the way to the Hospice Shop.

* * * * *

The morning regulars (or Breakfast Club as Brian called it) at El Marinero were perusing the local free newspaper, the Costa Reporter, whilst sitting inside the bar. A light shower had driven them inside and grey clouds promised more rain. A couple of stray tourists had joined them. Lynne was in a particularly bad mood that day, having had a row with Brian about time off. She wanted to close one day a week but he thought they should stay open. She was in one of her moods and he knew it was best to stay clear. She banged around in the kitchen, slamming saucepan lids and cupboard doors.

'Hello, hello!' exclaimed Mick, suddenly, 'Here we go again! Letters about the Winter Fuel Allowance.' The regulars all laughed, this topic came up every year about this time.

'Do you get the Winter Fuel here?' asked the unsuspecting

tourist.

'If you were in receipt of it before you came, yes. If not, no...'
Mick replied. Andrea chipped in,

'Phillip and I don't get it as we weren't old enough before we left
England..'

'And you weren't a household,' added Sandra, who knew they
had run away together. Andrea glared at her. Malc explained to the
newcomer.

'People in the UK hate us getting it, and yet it is our right, we
have paid in the same as them and we deserve it just as much.'

'But it doesn't get cold, does it?' asked unsuspecting tourist
number two.

'You what? You should have been here last Winter, it rained for
weeks and the wind...well...I'll tell you it was freezing in my house.'

'The problem is that these flats and houses were not built for bad
weather. We don't have central heating, like you do, or carpets on the
floors, we have cold marble floors, thin walls and single glazing. These
houses are built to stay cool in summer, not withstand the rigours of a
cold snap.' Phil explained

'And the cost of keeping cool in Summer is high,' said Malc, 'Air
con and fans to run.'

'But I can see the point,' said tourist number one, 'You don't
really qualify for Winter Fuel, it is not as though you will freeze to death
is it?'

'Could do, in the *campo*, ' said Sandra, 'They had frost, ruined
the mango trees.'

Jenny, the latest person to have a say in the morning debates,

151

explained.

'In 1997 the cost of fuel had gone through the roof but the state pension was still very low. Pensioners were struggling and lobbied the new labour Government to raise the pension so that could pay their heating bills. The Chancellor brought in the Winter Fuel Allowance for one year as an emergency measure, one off payment, but no Government has dared to scrap it since. If they had raised the pension as they should we would all be receiving it, as a right, and these questions wouldn't arise. It was only a sop to keep the pensioners quiet.'

Mick realised, at that point, that Jenny was a force to be reckoned with. His era as King of the Debating Society was coming to an end.

At that point Lynne stormed out of the kitchen and the female tourist touched her on the arm as she passed.

'Do you do food?' she asked.

'I do breakfasts and snacks,' Lynne stated.

'Oh you don't do lunch then? Spag Bol or something? You know, proper meals?'

'Madam,' said Lynne, patronisingly, 'If you want a proper meal then go next door to La Abuela's, I'm sure they can oblige, although I cannot recommend it as my husband and I have never had time to try it ourselves.' And with that remark she marched out of the door.

'Where are you going?' shouted Brian, embarrassed by her treatment of the customer.

'I'm going to find the shops, as I've never had a chance to look around them!' and she slammed the door behind her. Brian apologised to the customers, who then paid what they owed and left.

Chapter Fifteen

A Short Presentation

When Roger picked Julie up after her day at the Hospice Shop she seemed excited. She told him that the new Spanish volunteer, Bélen, had asked her if she would like to go on an outing, a coach trip.

'Where to?' Roger asked as the car headed up the road to their house.

'Torrebaja...right down the other end of the coast. I've heard it's a really nice old town, unspoilt, with a lovely old *torre,* watchtower.'

'Are you going then?'

'Yes. I put my name down. It's ever so cheap, a real Spanish outing, only ten euros including breakfast and lunch.'

'That is cheap..'

'Did you want to come?'

'Oh, no, you know what I'm like on buses, my knee always stiffens up and I can't walk when I get off. No, you go, you'll enjoy it.'

'There's only one snag and I promise you I didn't know until after I had said I'd go.'

'And what's that?'

'The bus leaves from the hotel at 6 am and we have to be there at 5.45 prompt or it will go without us.'

'That'll mean us getting up at half past four if we are to get down the mountain by 5.45.' Julie sounded sheepish, but she had thought it through.

154

'What we could do is stay a night in the hotel. Have dinner there and then in the morning you could stay in bed after I get up. Then you could take your time going back home.'

'Suddenly this cheap outing is getting more expensive.' Roger was not the kind to quibble about a few euros. He agreed to the idea and when they got home he rang the hotel and booked them in for one night. 'Don't forget the passports..' he told her, remembering their last hotel stay.

The evening before the excursion they dined in style in the hotel dining room. Julie ordered *solomillo* of pork, which is tenderloin, and was served a whole fillet swimming in a rich creamy pepper sauce. It was delicious but an enormous portion. Julie was one of those fortunate people who could eat whatever she liked without putting on so much as a pound, but this meal almost floored her, especially as she had had a substantial starter. They went to bed early, but Julie felt as though she had a boulder in her stomach and had to get up several times to try and walk it off. Had she been at home she could have taken something from the bathroom cabinet but they hadn't bothered to pack the collection of remedies which they took on longer trips. Consequently when the alarm went off at 5 am she had only had about three hours sleep, and the meal was still bloating out her stomach.

It was not quite light when she went down to where the coach was parked with its engine running, almost immediately below their balcony. Bélen was there, looking bushy-tailed and wide awake. Julie explained that they had stayed in the hotel and Bélen was amazed that they would pay out good money when they only lived half an hour's drive away. Julie couldn't be bothered to explain. Most of the coach party consisted of pensioners, and predominately women. There were a few old men amongst them. They looked like very old people, but Julie thought some of them probably weren't any older than she was, she supposed it was because they had had a hard life. They were all chattering away in indecipherable *Andaluz*, she could pick out very little *Castellaño*.

They got themselves onto the coach and there was a great deal of fuss made over who sat where. Old friends were greeting each other as though they hadn't seen one another for years, when in fact they probably saw each other every day. The bus left at 6 am on the dot and Julie settled back in her seat, expecting that once she woke up a bit the experience was going to be thoroughly enjoyable. Then she wondered why the coach had turned down the main road in the opposite direction from where it would join the motorway. In Spanish, as Bélen spoke very little English, she asked,

'Don't we go on the *Autovia*?'

'Yes, but there are one or two more people to pick up. They stopped a couple of hundred metres down the road and three more got on. Once again there was a palava over where they should sit, as it appeared everyone had a numbered ticket. They then went on another short distance and this time two women got off and everybody waited a long time. Bélen explained, 'They have to fetch Maria Dolores. She is old and slow.'

Maria Dolores lived in a tiny house sunken below street level a few yards up the road. The two women had gone to get her up and

156

dressed. Eventually they walked her slowly along the pavement, one either side of her, and between them they got her up the steps. Great cries of Maria! Maria! Went up from everybody as the old lady was settled in the front seat.

'Now we go to Ventamar, to collect some other people.'

Julie looked at her watch, it was 6.30 and they had hardly moved. After stopping for the last few souls the bus turned round and headed back the way they had come, then it suddenly did a right turn up the mountain road that led to Julie's house.

'Where are we going now?'

'To pick up Antonio and Carmen.'

'Where do they live?'

'In a *finca* near El Pozuelo.'

'That's near my house!' Julie exclaimed, realising that they could have picked her up at her door! As usual she avoided looking at the sheer drop over the edge of the twisting road. The old couple got on board and Bélen exclaimed, at last,

'Now we go to Torrebaja..' But to join the motorway they first had to go back down the mountain and through Orilla, passing the hotel where Julie had stayed the night. As they went by Julie caught a glimpse of Roger standing on the balcony, it was 7.15.

'Bélen, why didn't they pick these others up first and then we could have had an extra hour in bed?'

'Why? Didn't you enjoy going to all those houses? Why did you want more time sleeping?'

'What time did you get up?'

'About 4am. I had to see to the dogs and make my husband's

157

lunch.'

'Make his lunch? At that time?'

'It is of no consequence. If I don't make him lunch he does not eat.' Julie was astounded. No way would she cook a lunch in the middle of the night.

By this time she was feeling awful, her stomach felt so full and the movement of the bus was making her feel slightly sick. She hadn't had so much as a cup of tea. She took water from a bottle in her big handbag and sipped it. Then a woman got up and switched on the microphone that was provided for tour guides, and started to sing, in the kind of voice that needed no amplification, *coplas,* loud, flamenco style wailing. And they all joined in.

The noise level was appalling. Julie knew that Brits on outings could sing on their way back, at night, after a few drinks, but at this hour of the morning? On an empty stomach? Then the clapping started, the off-the-beat clapping that accompanied this type of music, with shrieks of *Olé! Olé!* Her head was starting to throb and she also felt she needed the toilet, as she was very regular and 8am was her time. The singing stopped but an old man got up to the sound of applause and screams of encouragement and started telling rude jokes in a rhyming format, the punch lines of which Julie couldn't understand, but which must have been hilarious as the noise of raucous laughter was deafening.

As the next contestant in this early morning talent contest sang a wailing, sad refrain with the microphone turned on full blast, Bélen turned to Julie.

158

'Now we have breakfast..' and the bus drew into the car park of a large *Salon de Celebraciones* where weddings, communions and other festivities were held. It was such a relief to get off the bus and feel the fresh, cool air on her face. Julie rushed to the toilet.

During a nice breakfast of toast and coffee Julie was fishing about in her handbag looking for paracetemol when Bélen explained,

'The reason this trip is so cheap is that we have to watch a short presentation. Not now, but at the next stop, when we stop for lunch.'

'Presentation of what?'

'Oh, some people will try and sell us things, but you do not have to buy.'

'What sort of things? Not timeshare? Not sunglasses or watches?'

'Oh, no. Kitchen things, things for the dining room, it doesn't take long. The company pays for our meals and we only pay for the bus, that is why it is so cheap.'

Back on the bus and the singing recommenced, louder than ever. Julie's head was throbbing now, even after taking the tablets she had managed to find, and the day seemed endless although it was only 10 o'clock. Bélen and the others, even the ancient Maria Dolores, were all wide awake and noisy and enjoying every minute.

At the next large *Salon de Celebraciones* they stopped for lunch, but first came the short presentation. They were all ushered into a large ballroom with long tables on three sides, tables were absolutely heaped with some sort of goods covered with gold velvet

159

cloths. Chairs, tightly packed in rows, as in a theatre, all faced forward. Julie carefully selected one on the end of a row, near the door, in case she needed to slip out to the toilet again which she felt was likely.

A smart young man in a business suit and tie stood centre stage and introduced himself, but he didn't just tell them his name, he told them where he came from, who his parents were, what they did for a living. He told them all about his brothers and sisters, nephews and nieces for which he got copious applause. He then introduced two young ladies in black pencil skirts and white blouses who each went through the same routine, the old people loving every minute of these detailed introductions. The fact that one of them had a brother who was a priest caused a ripple of excitement. Julie looked at her watch again, they had been there twenty minutes and it still hadn't started. The presenter then explained the quality of the products and at last the cloths were removed to reveal dozens of items, canteens of cutlery, dinner services, sets of crystal glassware, electrical goods and even a bed that would raise you up into a sitting position. Surely they wouldn't go through them all?

The first item was an electric paella pan. He listed every single type of meal it could be used for in detail, and finally, asked for thirty euros for it. Hands shot up, and when someone bought an item, the girls delivered it to them and the buyer got a round of applause. All this mystified Julie. These old people didn't look well off, they had come in their Sunday best clothes, and she had seen better on the rails of the Hospice Shop. One or two of them were sporting thick wool coats with fur collars and even though the temperature in the room was stifling they didn't take them off.

Two and a half hours later and the "short presentation" was still in progress and seemed to have no end. Old Maria Dolores had bought a canteen of gold plated cutlery with eighteen place settings. When she asked Bélen what the old lady would want it for and how could she afford it, she was told she would buy it in instalments, and that it was to impress her friends. So that was it! It was all down to creating the right impression, giving them a talking point, a reason for people to come round and look.   For that they would put themselves into debt. No British person would fall for this, Julie thought, they would see it as a scam.

Julie slipped out of the ballroom before they had finished and had a small glass of brandy at the bar. When Bélen joined her she explained that at the end of the presentation there had been a chance to buy one of everything for a knock down price, 'One day I will buy the lot!' she exclaimed, 'You can get it all for two thousand euros, my husband forbids me to do this, but one day I will. Can you imagine the envy of everybody, how they will applaud me?'

At last they went through for their lunch, which was *lomo* of pork with pepper sauce, almost identical to the dinner she'd had the night before. It was a nice meal but the very sight of it made Julie feel nauseous.

The bus headed off with everybody satisfied, full of food and having bought a collection of kitchenalia that would have done John Lewis' proud. It was all stowed in the luggage compartment. Julie wanted to go home. She had had enough. She closed her eyes while trying to decide whether it was too soon to take more Parecetamol. When she opened her eyes she got a shock, they were heading inland, up a mountain.

'I thought we were going to Torrebaja?'

'No, it is not the village of Torrebaja, but it is near it. Now we look at some animals.'

'Animals?' They were heading for Monte Salvaje, a Safari Park in a quarry half way up a mountain. The road got narrower and more steep, Julie closed her eyes again. Somebody went to the front of the bus, picked up the microphone and started to sing. The shrillness of her voice sawed through Julie's brain.

When the bus pulled into the car park and they alighted the village of Torrebaja could be seen twinkling on the coast. Through a haze of low cloud, in the far distance, it looked tiny, with a miniature watch tower like a charm on a bracelet. Up here it was cold, very cold, and Julie had not come prepared for this. It had been about 25 degrees in Orilla, here it was freezing. She had no socks on, very lightweight trousers, a short sleeved blouse and only a cardigan to keep her warm. She shivered. They were loaded onto trucks, regular open flatbed lorries that had been fitted with wooden benches. They were packed close together and then a piece of rope, that wouldn't stop anything falling off, was looped across the open sides. Julie was on one end, as Bélen insisted that she sit there so she could take better photographs. There was no chance of taking any photos at all as she dare not let go of the rail in front of her. Her camera stayed in her bag.

The trucks drove along narrow tracks only just the width of the wheelbase, it was terrifying. It was made even more harrowing by the

162

fact that the sheer drop into the quarry ended in a succession of pits containing lions, hippopotamus and other wild animals. If you survived the fall the beasts would get you. Julie had never been so frightened in her life, especially when the driver started playing about, taking the wobbly open trucks to the tops of ridges and then plunging them down vertical slopes so that everybody screamed.

It was at that point, when she saw all these old people actually enjoying this experience, when she weighed up the injustices of the 'short presentation' followed by this heart stopping roller coaster ride, when she added in the fact that none of them were a tiny bit weary or wanted to rest, that she knew her quest to be integrated into Spanish life was completely futile. She would have to remain English. And she was glad of it.

Chapter Sixteen

A Terrible Place to Die

When Brian got home that night he was surprised to find Lynne still up, sitting on the settee sipping a whiskey. He could see that she had something to say, and he had an inkling as to what it might be.

'Hello, still up? I am a bit early I know, there was nobody in so I closed.'

'Would you like a drink?'

'Yes, O.K., I didn't have my usual end of the night beer so...' Brian was adamant that neither of them drank while working, but he usually had a quick beer while he was closing up. She poured him a whiskey, and put ice in it. She had a grim expression on her face and this usually signalled some kind of major announcement was coming up. He braced himself.

'I've decided to go back. It's no good, I don't like it here. I can't get on with all these mad, sad people, and I'm sick to the back teeth of being locked up in that cubby hole frying bacon and chips.' She waited for him to say something, but what could he say, 'I need to get a life, and a proper job again,' she added.

'It was your idea to come. I didn't want to, I couldn't see it suiting you right from the off. If you want to go back, fair enough, but I'm staying.' She wasn't surprised.

'You will join me later, though?'

'Well, you can never say never, but as far as I am concerned the lease is a five year one and I shall see it out to the end.' Lynne took a long drink from the whiskey, draining the chunky glass, and topped it up from the bottle on the coffee table.

'If that's the way you want it...'

'Go back if you must, I'm not coming.'

'I've got a flight tomorrow morning at 10.15.' That was sudden, she had booked that today without speaking to him first, he thought that was a bit much, 'I had a look online and this one was available so I've booked it. Taxi is coming at 7am.'

'Well, you seem to have it all sewn up, what can I say?'

'You don't really like it here, do you? These crazy people and the heat and everything, what is there to like?' Time for the truth to come out.

'I absolutely love it. Never thought I would, mind. Thought I'd be the one booking the Easyjet back to Gatwick. And as for the crazy people, believe me in my job I've seen a few, drug addicts, thieves, murderers even, and you can't compare these ex-pats with the likes of them. These are good people, Lynne, a bit quirky some of them, a bit eccentric, but that's what I like. And I'm not bothered by the hours, I'm used to working during the night, remember?'

'But what will you do about the food?'

'I can cook a bacon sandwich or two, and if I can't cope I'll employ somebody.'

'Mick says if you take somebody on you have to pay Social Security and if they clear off it's almost impossible to get it stopped.'

'Then I'll do like all the other bars and pay cash in hand.'

'That's illegal! You wouldn't do that..'

'I might. There's no knowing what I'd do here that I wouldn't have done at home.'

'I'm sorry..' she said, 'We shouldn't have come...' and she started to look emotional. He put his arm round her and gave her a kiss.'

'Let's give it six months, you can come over and we'll see how the land lies. Where are you going to stay?'

'With Michelle until I find myself a place and a job.'

'You've thought it all out, haven't you?'

'Don't I always?' Lynne got up and went into the bedroom, 'Got to get up early, are you coming to bed?' He nodded, and drained his glass.

The next morning Lynne caught the taxi and he waved her off. He felt good. Her dislike of the lifestyle had been holding him back, now he could run the bar how he wanted. It was quite exciting, really. He went round the sparsely furnished flat and tidied up. He wouldn't be spending that much time in here, so it didn't matter that there were no home comforts. He didn't feel guilty, either, that he was glad she had gone. All those years when he was always working and when he got time off she would be away on one of her promotional events. They had lost touch with each other. She thought that being here, in each other's company day after day would bring them back together again but it had shown up their marriage for what it was, nothing more than a stale friendship. They weren't the same people that had married in a rush in 1977, because she was expecting their daughter, Michelle, not the same silly people who once thought they were in love.

He left the block and walked over to the bar, a bit late, but, what the hell! He was heaving up the heavy metal shutters when a voice at his elbow said,

'Has Lynne gone to the U.K?' It was Andrea, with Phil in tow.

'How on earth...she has only just set out in the taxi...she is barely at the airport..'

'Jimmy rang me..you know Jimmy,' he didn't but he let her carry on, 'Jimmy saw her struggling with her bags in departures. She said she had gone back for good, is that right?' No need to cover it up, Brian thought.

'Yes, she couldn't settle here. I didn't try to stop her.'

'Oh, I am sorry...' They followed him inside.

'You won't be going, then?' asked Phil.

'No, you won't get rid of me that easily!'

'What's that noise?' asked Andrea, who had ears like a bat. They stopped talking and listened, there was a faint tapping noise and a weak voice crying,

'Hello? Hello?'

'It's the toilet!' Andrea deduced, 'Somebody's locked in the ladies like I was on quiz night...' They went to the toilet door and Brian shouted, stand back, and put his shoulder to it. It wouldn't budge so he and Phil tried together, counting to three and then charging with all their might.

The door burst in and there, flattening herself against the wall, stood Trish, looking limp and exhausted. She pushed past them heading for the front door.

'Trish! I didn't even see you come in..'

'I've been in there all night, darling...nowhere to lay down but at

167

least I had an en suite..' she shook her long hair and rubbed her smudged ink black eyelids.

'Do you want a coffee? Cup of tea or...'

'No, thanks, darling. I just want to go home,' and she wobbled off in the direction of the Paseo.

These mad, sad people Lynne had called them. Every day was an experience, every day was unpredictable, that's what he liked about it all.

* * * * *

Pat sat at the usual table in Emilio's. There was no sign of Keith. She had his number now and so she could ring him, but she was nervous about it, why hadn't he let her know if he wasn't coming? The other week when it rained he gave her a call to check, that's what they had decided they would do. Emilio came over and took her empty cup away.

'Your friend? He not come?' she shook her head. Oh, this was ridiculous, she fished her phone out of the bag strung across her body and found his name in the mobile's phone book. The phone rang four or five times and she was just about to hang up when a woman answered.

'Hello?'

'Oh, hello...I was looking for Keith..'

'I'm Pippa, his daughter.' Well, that explains it, Pat thought, a surprise visit from his daughter.

'I'm Pat, a friend of his.'

'I'm sorry, Pat, but I've some bad news. Dad passed away last Friday.'

'What?'

'Had a heart attack it seems, his neighbour found him and the Police rang me. I flew over to sort things out. I'm at the flat now clearing his stuff out. Do you know where it is?'

'Yes.. it's the...' Pat started to shake violently, she couldn't believe it.

'I can tell you're upset. Come round, I'll meet you at the back gates of the Monaco block, OK?'

'I'll come now.' Pat fumbled in her purse to pay Emilio but dropped the money on the floor, he helped her pick it up, 'He's dead,' she told him, 'He's dead!'

Back gates of the Monaco block? But he lived in the Buena Vista? She didn't understand this, she didn't understand any of it. He was fine last week, last Wednesday, how could this have happened? She made her way along the back lanes that passed her own building to the shabby Monaco block. It had been built in the seventies and was long overdue for a "reform". Chunks of concrete were missing from some of the balconies, black streaks stained the once white walls. It was a tatty block, what was Pippa doing there when Keith lived in the beautiful Buena Vista?

She reached the rusty iron gates and a tall woman with Keith's blue eyes and pale blonde hair let her through.

'I'm so sorry to have to break the news like that. Were you

169

close?' I loved him, thought Pat, but daren't say it.

'I was.... fond of him.' Pippa led her inside, up in a rickety lift and along the straight grey corridors. She unlocked the heavy wooden panelled door of flat number 3F. It was a sad little room with shabby furniture and horrible wrought iron light fittings. Pat sank onto the hard sofa. There were boxes everywhere. Pippa didn't seem that distressed.

'I've had to box up all his things, the landlord's only given me to the end of the week.'

'Landlord?'

'Yes, he didn't own this place, it is only rented, cheapest he could get, probably.'

'Poppy! Where's Poppy?' Pat looked round for signs of the animal.

'Who's Poppy?'

'His dog, his little dog.' Pippa looked as bemused as she did.

'Dad didn't have a dog.' It got stranger and stranger, why had he lied to her? All those stories about Poppy and Esteban and playing chess on the lovely curved verandah of the Buena Vista with its stunning sea view and beautiful gardens. She felt she had to get some air and went out on the small balcony, she leaned on the rusty railing and it wobbled, she drew back. Pippa went to make some tea. Now Pat didn't know what to make of all this, he was a liar and a cheat and she had thought so much of him.

She came back in and sat down.

'Would you like a souvenir? Take anything you like, what about this?' She held up a framed photograph of a young man in Army uniform. So handsome.

170

'No, it's of your dad, you keep it. When is the funeral?'

'Oh, I'm afraid it's all over, you know how they are here, they want it all over and done with in 24 hours. I had him cremated, then I'll take him back. You wouldn't believe the paperwork.'

'Oh, I would, I would. This is a great country to live in but it is a terrible place to die.' Pat took the mug of tea from her with shaky hands. 'Who found him? Esteban?'

'Sorry?'

'His neighbour, Esteban?'

'His neighbour is Mrs whatshername...Garcia.. and on the other side is an empty flat.' Pippa must have thought she was talking about a different man altogether. Pat drank the tea and tried to gather her thoughts, but they were whirling about and colliding in her brain.

'So you were fond of Dad, then?' Pippa asked. It was then that the waters of her grief broke, and Pat started to cry. She sobbed uncontrollably, it all gathered itself up, all the misery and injustice of Bob leaving her and now Keith. It seemed everybody she had any affection for went the same way, her darling baby son dying in her arms when he was only a week old, her mother dying young. Were they all in some paradise waiting for her, or was it just fate that things kept happening like this? She knew she would never see them again. Once she had started she couldn't stop, she wailed and sniffled until her eyes were red raw. Pippa's eyes were filling up too, her staunch reserve was faltering. She held her, as though she was her own daughter, until there was no energy left in either of them. Then Pat took a deep breath and stood up.

'I'm going now. Thank you, ' she said, sniffing and pulling

171

together what fragments remained of her self esteem.

'Are you sure you won't take a memento? I'm throwing it all out.'

They went into the small hallway and there by the phone was a little basket with keys, mint imperials, string and the detritus of a man's pocket tossed into it. Under the key ring was a receipt. Pat, even with her blurred vision, spotted that the receipt was printed with the words "New Yang Chinese Restaurant". She pulled it carefully from the basket and glanced quickly at the items listed, then folded it neatly in half.

'I'd like to keep this...' she said, putting it into the breast pocket of her shirt blouse.

'Are you sure?'

'Yes. This is my memento. Thank you for telling me about your father,' and she let herself out of the flat.

She almost ran through the unimpressive gardens of the Monaco. There was an old swimming pool, drained, because it was showing signs of a crack. She skirted round it and headed for the back gate. She searched for the button that opened the gate and as she pulled it open she almost walked into a short bald man with a very shiny brown head and smiling eyes. He had a wooden box under one arm and a dog's lead in the other hand. At the end of the lead was a small, whitish dog with one lob-sided ear and a brown spot on its backside. She stared at the dog for a minute, and then, not stopping to think if the man spoke any English or not, she asked.

'Excuse me, is that your dog?'

'Yes,' he said, 'That is my Amapola.' Then, seeing her bloodshot eyes and blotchy cheeks he asked.

'Were you a friend of Keith's?'

'Yes,' she said, 'You do know ...' He knew full well, he nodded.

'It is very sad. I was very good friend with him, he used to come round to my house two or three times a week to play chess. He loved to sit on the terrace of my apartment at the Buena Vista.' Suddenly it all made sense.

'What did you say your dog was called?'

'Amapola, it means Poppy in English. And I am Esteban.' He gave her a little bow and offered his hand, she shook it.

It was all real, it was all true! There was a Poppy and Esteban and games of chess on the curved terrace of the Buena Vista! The only thing that wasn't true was Keith's address, he had been ashamed to say that he lived in the run down Monaco block. It was very nearly true, he hadn't lied to her! Well, not much.

'I am taking the chess set back to his daughter,' Esteban explained, 'Mrs Garcia said she had come.'

'Oh, no, don't do that,' said Pat, 'She will only throw it out. You keep it, I am sure he would want you to have it, please, keep it.' He thought for a minute and agreed, checking,

'If you are sure.'

'Absolutely. Did he mention me? I'm Pat?'

'Oh yes, many times. He was always talking of you. We are both alone now, you and me, is that not right?' She started to well up again, but fought it back. 'Perhaps I could help you? If you need a translation, help with papers, anything?' He seemed such a nice, kind man.

173

'I am learning Spanish, but I am not very good,' she confessed.

'I can help you with that! You could come to the Buena Vista, you could practice with me. Please, I am an honourable man, you do not need to worry.'

'Oh, no, I'm not worried, I would like that. Or you could come to my flat. Do you like cake? I make very good cake.' He said that he did and then took out a scrap of paper, probably a bus ticket, found a pen, and leaning on the chess set he wrote his name and number. 'You ring me when you want to come. No hurry.' he said, 'When you are ready.'

She took the little square of paper and folded it, then placed it in the same pocket as the receipt, next to her heart. They smiled, she patted the dog and each turned towards their own home.

'*Hasta luego..*' she said, clearly, 'See you soon.' And when she did, she would grab it with both hands.

Carole Hart, August 2010

SPANISH GLOSSARY

Although in almost all cases I have explained the Spanish words used in the text, here is a list of those words and expressions that are mentioned.

A

abierto	open (boquerones abierto: anchovies opened up and boned out)
abuela	Grandmother
almejitas blancas	an invention of mine meaning "little white clams"
amapola	poppy
Andaluz	the dialect of Andalucia
autentico	authentic
Autovia	motorway
ay – eee!!!	Spanish shriek of excitement, as in football match

B

barato	cheap
basura	rubbish
bata	loose dress worn like a dressing gown
bolsa	carrier bag
bolso	handbag
boquerones	anchovies
buenas dias	good day/morning

C

café con leche	coffee with milk
calamares	squid, usually cut into rings
campeones del Mundo	champions of the World

campo	inland (away from the coast) usually up the mountains, literally "field"
carta	menu
casetas	bars at the féria
Castellaño	official Spanish language
Centro Commercial	shopping mall
chorizo	spicy sausage
churros	extruded breakfast doughnut for dipping into hot chocolate/coffee
combinado	drinks combined, i.e rum & coke, gin & tonic
communidad	community of owners
compresas	sanitary towels
coplas	flamenco type songs
cortado	coffee with a little milk, literally "cut off"
Cuba libre	rum and coke (Free Cuba)

D

denuncia	report to the police denouncing someone
deposito	deposit

E

embutidos	cooked meats, sausages, salamis etc.
estoy	I am
escalera	ladder, steps or staircase
extranjero/a	foreigner

F

farola	street lamp
féria	annual fair
fijado	fixed
finca	farm, smallholding

G

garbanzos	chick peas
gazpacho	cold soup, usually cucumber and tomato
golosinas	sweets, usually chews or jellies
Guardia Civil	National paramilitary police

H

hasta luego	until the next time
hola	hello

L

leche manchada	very milky coffee, literally "stained milk"
Ley Horizontal	the law concerning the administration of community blocks
Liga (La)	the football league
lo siento	I am sorry (for it)
lomo	pork loin

M

marinero	sailor
Miercoles	Wednesday (not Meercolas!)
muy mal	very bad

N

naranja natural	natural squeezed orange juice
no cambiar	no exchange
no pase nada	it's no problem
no regalo para el	no gift for him

P

pan tostado	toast
Paseo (Marítimo)	the sea front promenade where one takes a "paseo", a walk

pippas	sunflower seeds
piratas	three quarter length trousers
precios	prices

Q

que pasa?	What's going on?

R

racion	a ration, plate of food, often shared
residencia	permit of residence

S

Salon de Celebraciones	banqueting hall
Semana Santa	Holy Week, Easter
sin alcohol	without alcohol (beer or wine)
sobresada	Mallorcan spreading sausage, a kind of flavoured dripping
solomillo	pork fillet
soy	I am

T

tapas	small plates of food served with drinks
tipico	typical
todavia	on going, still going on
torre	watchtower
tortilla	omelette

V

vestido de volantes	frilly dress, as in flamenco dancing
verde	green

Z

zero zero	drink with no alcohol (beer or wine)

THANKS

My thanks to

Sue for help with the proof reading

Mike for the expressions "dust distributor" and "gene of forethought"

Bernie for the "compresas" and "nun with crocodile" stories

Beryl for the "three weeks to live" story

Margaret and Roger for the "stuck on the step" story

Carol and Murray for the "van to Bulgaria" story

Lightning Source UK Ltd.
Milton Keynes UK
UKOW051207101011

180075UK00001B/182/P

9 781907 407512